The Broken Roads End

The Broken Roads End

FACT OR FICTION?

CAROL L. STRAYER-MCTURNER

THE BROKEN ROADS END
FACT OR FICTION?

Copyright © 2017 Carol Strayer.

All rights reserved. No part of this book may be used or reproduced by any means, graphic, electronic, or mechanical, including photocopying, recording, taping or by any information storage retrieval system without the written permission of the author except in the case of brief quotations embodied in critical articles and reviews.

This is a work of fiction. All of the characters, names, incidents, organizations, and dialogue in this novel are either the products of the author's imagination or are used fictitiously.

iUniverse books may be ordered through booksellers or by contacting:

iUniverse
1663 Liberty Drive
Bloomington, IN 47403
www.iuniverse.com
1-800-Authors (1-800-288-4677)

Because of the dynamic nature of the Internet, any web addresses or links contained in this book may have changed since publication and may no longer be valid. The views expressed in this work are solely those of the author and do not necessarily reflect the views of the publisher, and the publisher hereby disclaims any responsibility for them.

Any people depicted in stock imagery provided by Thinkstock are models, and such images are being used for illustrative purposes only.
Certain stock imagery © Thinkstock.

ISBN: 978-1-5320-1465-9 (sc)
ISBN: 978-1-5320-1466-6 (e)

Library of Congress Control Number: 2017900000

Print information available on the last page.

iUniverse rev. date: 12/30/2016

Chapter 1

Lethal Obsessions

The smell was something that had been etched in his mind forever. Even before Officer Rusty Jackson arrived on the scene, he knew it to be the stench of decaying flesh. In the 10 years he'd been working for the Clay Police Department, he had never seen nor smelled anything quite like this. What seemed to be a woman's body, lay prone on the rocks near the shore. Thanks to the weather's warm trend, flies, maggots, growth, fish, and animals had a chance to ravish the body, leaving hair, bones, and flesh looking like patchwork gone bad. There hadn't been a report of anyone missing in years, but with the many remote areas along this 66-mile-long river, the body's origin was a mystery only the river knew. Due to the economic conditions, many people erected makeshift camps along the river they called home. In the past months, with the rain and the snow, as well as a freeze and thaw, the river's flooding would reveal many secrets. This secret however, was one of the most horrendous.

Officer Jackson had gotten the call from a fisherman who had been boating on the river on this warm winter day. He claimed to have seen the body on the shore and noticed the foul odor. This area was one of the many remote areas along the Elk River, but Officer Jackson, the only police officer with a horse, had little problem reaching the scene. Because of its out of the way location, OFC Jackson was elected to the job of cordoning off the area with crime scene tape, and waiting for backup. He had radioed his position upon his arrival, and with an ETA of 20 minutes by foot, he and his horse were left alone with the body. The fisherman, who had called from a pay phone, gave his information, but understandably refused to return to the area. The Clay County Sheriff Dale Taylor, obtained all pertinent information and would follow up with the corner and another officer on the scene.

"Jasmine," Rusty said gently to his horse. "I wish you weren't as sure footed as you are. Seems to me, we get the worst of the worst out here in the boonies. I been thinkin, I might retire you. Not saying we're not ridin' anymore, but I'm a thinkin you need to become an occasional trail rider. That way we won't be gettin these disgustin' assignments."

Rusty Jackson loved riding Jasmine, but now that she was fifteen years old, he thought it was best to give her a break from the rugged walks along the Elks riverbanks. Instead, he wanted to keep her closer to home and travel the familiar trails of the mountain he had grown to love. She had worked well with him for the past twelve years, but for his own reasons, he felt it was time to retire her.

Jasmine was a beautiful Appaloosa, who stood thirteen hands high. Her gray spots outweighed the white, leaving her looking a dusty gray from a distance. At three years old she was a high spirited and powerful mare with rippling muscles. Rusty learned resistance training which developed his natural horsemanship. With this, he and Jasmine became one. A well working machine. With little direction, Jasmine knew where to go and what to do. Thus, they became a highly sought after pair when traversing the mountainous terrain of West Virginia.

An afternoon of babysitting the corpse ended with the rustling of dry branches and muffled conversation coming from the woods. The approach of Rusty's comrades was loud enough to scare anything hiding in the woods such as any wildlife or possible suspects. There was one saying known well in the mountains of West Virginia. Always, and above all, "BE CAREFUL!"

"Rusty!" Sheriff Taylor called from the thickets that lie between them. "Did you see an opening we can get through?" Sheriff Taylor had been in this area before, many years ago, but with the constant change in the terrain from flooding that occurs at least three times a year, he had to find new ways to reach the river each time.

"Go around about 50 feet. Seems to thin out there." Rusty knew this area well. He had mentally prepared for Sheriff Taylor's arrival by scanning the area beforehand. It took only a few minutes longer before Sheriff Taylor, OFC Cummings, and Dr. Jake Holmes, the county coroner, were overcome by the rancid odor, even before seeing the body.

"Oh shit!" Officer Cummings was the first to react.

. "Ew ee musky! This one's been here a while!" Sheriff Taylor knew the smell as he had discovered many bodies in his years working as sheriff. Not all bodies were homicides however; some people who lived in these out of the way areas, were only occasionally found deceased.

"Rusty, you didn't touch anything, right?" Doc Holmes asked at the start of his investigation. He knew he hadn't, but for the record, he had to ask.

Rusty was worn out, but still hadn't lost his sense of humor. "Well Doc, I had taken a ride on Jasmine to look at the scenery, but she, the corpse, got a little hard to hold with her flesh falling off her ass onto the saddle." Rusty stopped with the imagery. "Sorry, no Doc, I touched nothin'"

"Go figure, finally found a woman and she's fallen to pieces over you!" Doc Holmes shook his head. Doc had a sense of humor too. It was one thing that helped keep him sane. He never meant any disrespect to the deceased, nor did Rusty, it was just a survival mechanism. By adding humor to a difficult situation, the task at hand was easier to handle.

Rusty did a great job placing the police tape around the scene. Now, OFC

Cummings began to photograph the area and the body before anyone touched the body. Camera flashes and the sound of a shutter began the discovery phase of the investigation.

After a roll of film was emptied at the scene of discovery, Doc Holmes began his own discovery process. He removed his small cassette recorder and began his notes.

"Female, between the age of thirty and thirty-five. Appears to have been washed down stream; origin unknown. Found lying along the shore of the Elk River, prone on the stones approximately…" He paused the tape.

"Rusty, how far from Clay would you say we are?"

"We're about six miles up Elk, four miles as the crow flies." Rusty knew that answer with his extensive knowledge of the area.

"Good enough." He nodded his head and continued. "Six miles up the Elk River from Clay. The body shows decay, but no definite time of death now due to the fluctuating temperatures the past few weeks. Clothing on the body consists of blue jeans, which are torn in many areas, a white cotton T-shirt, also torn in many areas. There are no shoes with the body. Hair color appears to be a natural blonde," Doc Holmes paused the tape. "Cummings, where is the spray paint? Let's outline her so I can flip her over."

Cummings scrambled over the rocky shoreline, fumbling in his backpack for the quick dry fluorescent orange paint. He popped the lid and began to outline, starting at the top of the head, and sprayed clockwise around the arm, which was extended at a 35° angle, and the legs which were spread slightly, then around the other arm which was at a 60° angle. To Cummings, this was the easy part. The next part was what he always dreaded, turning a decayed corpse.

After a few minutes, Doc instructed, "Now Rust, get the head, Cummings, the legs, I'll control the torso." He knew where to position everyone. As they all took their positions, Doc began his count. "One, two, three." The fear was palpable right before the turn; the fear she would fall apart. No one ever spoke of this fear, but all braced for it. With effortless motion, the three flipped her to her back, without incidence.

"What the hell?" Sheriff Taylor was the first to see the face.

"Who would do something like that?" Rusty knew it wasn't a botched medical procedure.

OFC Cummings froze in horror. He felt a wave of nausea as he saw the disfigurement, but knew he had to keep it under control.

Doc Holmes knew the reason for what they saw. Someone wanted to hide the identity. The woman's jaw showed signs of having her teeth removed erratically, with bits of roots remaining. This removed any chance of using dental record for identification. He looked at her hands, now facing upwards. Each fingertip was removed as well, having been burned off, leaving no chance for fingerprint identification. *I'm surprised he left her hair,' Doc* thought to himself. *Thank God, we have DNA. The only problem now is the missing person report. Often, they don't worry about adults.*

"Doc, you ever see anything like this?" Sheriff Taylor asked after absorbing the horrific scene.

"Nope," was all he said.

"Some son-a-bitch needs to fry for this one." Cummings finally got his voice back. "You think he's from the area?" His disgust turned to anger. "I'd love to run into this one. Give me a chance and I'd tear him a new asshole! Anyone, anyone, who'd do something like that…"

"All right Cummings, that's enough." Sheriff Taylor felt the same repulsion, but he knew it voicing his opinion wouldn't help the situation.

Rusty stood shaking his head in disbelief. Here laid a young woman, who, if her face was intact, was pretty compared to many of the hillbilly women he had met. "You think she was from around here, Doc?"

"No telling at this point. We'll have to check the missing persons list when we get back. I couldn't imagine no one reporting her missing." No matter how long he had been doing this type of work, Doc would never understand how a person could commit such a ghastly crime. How, where, when, and why were the questions to be answered now, and it would take all he had to find a solution.

"We are going to need a body bag Cummings. Lay it out while Doc finishes. "Reckon we won't have any trouble putting her in without her coming apart will we Doc?" Sheriff Taylor asked.

Cummings and Jackson were the designated helpers for this job. Doc didn't want too many hands touching the corpse. Although he hated the responsibility, Sheriff Taylor was prepared to put his gloves on to help if it need be.

Doc Holmes knew Taylor loathed touching carcasses of any kind, and that this was a rare opportunity to let him help. "You know, Dale, those gloves of yours ain't touched anything like this before. Why don't you take Cumming's place and have a feel? You'd be surprised at how much it feels like Jell-O."

Cummings stood quickly, more than willing to relinquish his place. "Go-ahead Sheriff, I was getting tired of stooping anyways." In on the ribbing, Cummings stood to remove his gloves.

"Sure Sheriff, show us how you'd do it? We are new to this type of work ya know." Rusty said, adding his two cents.

"Yeah, yeah, I get it. Seeing me touch her would tickle you pink, wouldn't it? I think y'all can handle it. I didn't get this badge by listening to the likes of you." Sheriff Taylor said as he backed away knowing they finally had their shot at harassing him over his phobia. "I hope your happy cause when it's your turn, for the pesterin', I'm gonna be first in line."

The group laughed at his comment. If not for the absurdity of the remark, the job at hand would be unbearable.

The task was finished, per protocol as daylight diminished. Rusty, with the help of the others, loaded the body across Jasmine's hind quarters and secured it for the ride to Doc Holmes' station wagon. The responsibility for finding the murderer had just begun. Hopes were high there would be no further bodies found before justice was served, but years would pass before it came to fruition.

Rusty mounted Jasmine as they walked out of the remote area towards their vehicles. Not a word was spoken as they went out of sight. Rusty, clicked and Jasmine responded knowing her master's commands. "Girl, I promise, this is the last one."

Chapter 2

So, it Begins Again.

It was Friday, July 26, 2002, another hot and humid summer. Not much different from the years before, except this was the day the planet aligned at the perfect angle and he waited for his next victim. The alignment occurred in this precise angle every three years. Although it was never on the same day or month, by his calculations, today was the day. He sat in his usual position at his usual establishment, knowing he needed to be alert for destiny to walk through the door.

Just need one more Insurance presentation to meet my weekly quota, and here's the weekend, she thought. Kathy was tired of the No's. *Families, couples, or individuals with children are all she needed.* But the weekend beat her in the end. The phone, ringing, disrupted her thoughts.

"American insurance company, this is Kathy, how may I help you?" She answered, enthusiastically hoping for a chance at a sale.

"Kathy, could you help me out?" Said a familiar voice.

"Shari, what's going on?" Kathy asked, knowing full well it was more family drama. Shari was her first cousin, had experienced enough, and created the rest. Still, all drama not created carried through to the created; no one knew which was which.

"Kathy, our car is broken down at moms and she said she would pick John up after work. Now she changed her mind and won't. What time do you get off tonight?"

Maybe my next presentation, Kathy thought? "What time does he get off work?" She countered.

"He gets out at 5:30, but is you can get off a little earlier we can go together."

"Here's the deal, I will show you the insurance I feel is the best one available in your price range." Kathy knew they couldn't buy now, but she knew when they could, they would do business with her. "Let me get my things, and I will be there within the hour."

"You're a life saver Kathy. And yes, you can."

Kathy saw it was now 4:30, and give or take five, she would arrive in time to sit at the lodge for at least one Coors light. The lodge and the lake were once owned by her great-grandfather and held many fond memories. Beaver Lake, full of lily pads, which had overgrown since the new owners took over, was summers of fun. Shari and Kathy enjoyed many summers with their grandmother, who had since passed. Shari was now a proud homeowner at the lake, within yards of her mother's home, and the grandparents Homestead. Even closer to the Homestead of her great grand-parents. She continues the Sones' presence at the lake.

The ride to the lake seemed quicker than usual. No outrageous traffic on the interstate and no farm tractors to slow her. The music she selected for the ride was her favorite country station with Alan Jackson's *"Prop Me Up Beside the Jukebox."* Beer drinking music was what she wanted to hear. It had been a good week. Just over a month ago, Carl moved out. And, to top it off, it would have been her 12-year anniversary two days after. Kathy was never a drinker, but tonight it would change. Tonight, she'll give in to temptation and the sky's the limit.

As Kathy made the turn onto Beaver Lake Road, she noticed the cars at the Lodge. The parking lot was filled so Kathy proceeded to the last house on the east side of the lake. Shari waited on the porch. The house, a two-story with an open basement, set on the shore of the lake with the porch overhanging the water. Shari's husband and children had cleared the lily pads around the shore and made the porch into a fisherman's sanctuary.

Shari quickly gathered her purse and descended the steps two at a time. She was dressed in a black low cut cotton shirt and tight jeans. Shari looked like she was on the prowl instead of picking her husband up from work. This was nothing new. She often hid behind make-up and tightfitting clothing.

"Let's rock and roll!" She called out as she climbed into Kathy's car. She knew exactly where the seat lever was to slide the seat back, and within seconds there was a click and a slam. "Where do you want to go?"

"Well, the Lodge is full, so why not go to Larry's Inn? We've got to go there to pick up John anyways."

"Cool! Let's do it!" Shari was more than willing. Life was never easy for Shari. Molested and raped by her step-father, didn't end until the birth of Angie. Story has it, there was a boyfriend. No one spoke about.

Kathy, knowing the family's history, knew the best thing to do was to crank up the music and proceed quickly to the designated bar. A familiar route only fifteen minutes away. A right turn, then left, then another right. Again, the country lyrics, "*Rearview Mirror Torn Off, We ain't Looking Back,*" echoed in the car. They sang along with the radio with occasional bursts of laughter when they sang the same words wrong. They both agreed, they knew the words they wanted to sing!

As they approached the Inn, again it looked like a used car lot, "Is there a convention in town?" asked Kathy.

"Not that I know of." Shari replied.

Kathy pulled into the back of the parking lot. Her Saturn slipped easily into a small space between the telephone pole and a black Harley, which attracted her attention. As the two climbed out of the car, Kathy looked at Shari and said, "I am going to get us free drinks tonight. Sit back and watch!"

"Don't you have any money?" Shari asked fearfully.

"Yeah but this will be fun!"

"Thank God, I was hoping to borrow $10 until John gets his check cashed." Shari hated to admit she didn't have any money, but having three children and one income, it was paycheck to paycheck. Today, being payday, Kathy understood more than Shari knew.

"Shari, you're covered." Kathy reassured her. "Besides, we don't need any money girl. Watch the pro."

Kathy was dressed in a black spaghetti strap dress with matching black and white jacket and was still in the selling mode. The first thing she needed to do was to sell herself. Personality, personality, personality was the motto. She devised a plan. Using stereotypical observation, she would look for the Harley driver. Tattoos, skullcaps, Harley shirt, young, old, or mid-lifer, all were fair game. As she walked into the bar, Kathy scanned the room. There were three guys with ball caps, none with Harley emblems or logo. There were T-shirts galore, but again no luck. Kathy walked towards the back of the bar with Shari in tow. Suddenly she spotted the one she would approach. He had a skullcap with confederate flags printed on each side. He appeared to be a mid-lifer, in his 50s. *Bingo!* She thought as she approached him confidently.

"Is that your Harley in the parking lot?" She spouted uninhibited.

"Wish it were." He spoke with a deep southern drawl. He turned to face Kathy, smiled his best smile, and flashed his deep blue eyes her way. *Now this is a challenge!* he thought.

"You must be wearing this to hide your bald spot, aren't you?" She smiled her best smile and flashed her blue eyes at him and pulled his skullcap off his head.

"Nope, you must be mistakin' me for my brother!" He responded as he brushed his hair back with one hand. It was locks of gray and dark red highlights and only a small bald area. He smiled at her and her nerve. No one who knew him ever pulled a dew rag from his head. *You're lucky you're a woman,* he thought. *And may be the right one.*

"Whatcha drinking?" He asked.

"Well, even though you don't own that Harley," Kathy said. She looked over at Shari, "Shari, how long we have?"

"About a half hour," Shari replied without missing a beat.

"What you want to drink?" Kathy asked without looking back at Mr. Harley,

"Rum and Coke?"

Turning back to Mr. Harley at the bar, "Order me a rum and coke, and a Coors light draft." Kathy knew if he chose not to pay, she was ready to pull out her money.

"Who is that pretty lady behind you?" Mr. Harley questioned.

"That is my cousin. We're meeting her husband here after work., She responded cautiously. "We're drinking, I'm buying!"

"Bull-butter. New! Get me another, a rum and coke, and a Coors light draft for my lady friends."

The bartender, a young long-haired blonde, responded quickly to his request. She became fond of Deuce on the first day he started at the Inn. He asked her for her name but failed to hear a thing after "I'm new." From that time on, he nicknamed her New. And since the pipeliners were in the area, her tips doubled to tripled so she'd answer to anything.

"What was I thinkin'," Deuce stood off his stool. "Ladies?" waving one arm towards the empty stools, he watched as Kathy directed Shari to the further stool from him, and sat instantly onto the stool he was just sitting on. He stood to her right, at the end of the bar, knowing *this could be the one.* He lit a cigarette, drawing ever so slowly as he watched Kathy adjust in her seat. *She is a tall cup of water: red hair, blue eyes, and a nice body.*

"So, what are you doing all dressed up in this shit-ass bar so far away from civilization? You meeting your husband here too?" Deuce was fishing.

"Well, I just got off work. I am an insurance agent. Do you need life insurance?" Kathy knew better, but it was worth a shot and delayed giving the relationship answer.

As the bartender set the rum and Coke in front of Shari, Kathy took a chance and gave her a wink of success. Her beer followed, as well as his can of Bud light. *I still got it!* She thought, *even after all these years.*

"What is the name of the insurance company? I might already have some." Deuce had no intention of buying insurance. With his type of work, he was so insured that he was worth more dead than alive.

"American insurance company." Kathy stated proudly.

"Seriously? My cousin, out of West Virginia, works for them!" He lied. *The games begin.* Leaning on the bar with his elbow, "How long you been working for them?" he asked quizzically.

"I've only worked three months with them, but I worked for Ultimate Insurance

Company before that." Kathy said as she sipped her beer, evaluating the southerner beside her. He was robust. Kathy saw a man in a Carhartt coat and pants with a lot of miles worn into them. His hair was gray with dark red highlights from his youth. His mustache was more red than gray. His tan showed where his glasses had been worn. He was a working man with an odd name.

"I heard the bartender call you Deuce. Where are you from?" She asked. She always loved a deep voice with a southern drawl, and he had one. She hadn't heard one since Texas. "And where did you get that name?"

"Well, let me tell you. I've been all over the world, but I call West Virginia my home.

Born and raised. Got four brothers, Chuck, Paul, Mike, and Tim. My name comes from them. That's another story. I was born Frank Allen James, but everyone calls me Deuce."

"Was that your brother sitting here?", New asked.

Recalling the conversation, she just had, Kathy turned to see if she could spot the man New pointed to. There was a blonde-haired cowboy sitting at the table in the far corner. He looked to be in his 20s. He was very good looking and sported a mustache.

"Mike!" Deuce yelled to the man at the table and waved him to come over. "No, but he lives near me. He worked with me on the pipeline going across the state."

"What the fuck do you want old man? Didn't you see me making my moves?" Mike protested, just as he saw Kathy smiling at him. "Pardon me, ma'am," he said, tipping his white cowboy hat. "He and I go way back. He wouldn't know what to do if I didn't give him a hard time."

Where you working right now?" Kathy asked as Mike came behind her to address Deuce.

The Broken Roads End

"Mike, this is… You never told me your name." He would finally put a name to her.

"Kathy. And this is Shari." Kathy noticed that she had barely talked to her since sitting down. Shari sat nearly drooling as Mike came and stood beside Deuce.

"Glad you remembered I was sitting here." Shari tapped her cup, in need of another rum and Coke.

"Looks like you need another," Deuce interjected. "New!" he called. "Another round here!" Deuce pulled a large wad of money from his pocket to pay for the drinks. He was holding two weeks' pay in his hand, about three thousand dollars, give or take a hundred. He pulled out a one-hundred-dollar bill and slapped it on the bar in front of him.

They like a man with money, he thought as he placed his money back into his pocket. *Now, is she available?* Kathy peaked his curiosity.

"So, should I be worried about your husband or boyfriend, pounding me because I'm buying you drinks?" Deuce asked, hoping for the response he wanted. *I need you to be single, but either way, you're the one.*

Kathy knew she would have to admit her relationship status eventually and unconsciously bowed her head to respond to his question. Shari overheard the question and interjected, "She's divorced." Kathy turned to her cousin with an *I was going to tell him eventually,* look.

"Yeah, yeah, I'm actually separated. He moved out." Kathy wasn't ready to accept it. The marriage had become more of a roommate situation for the last ten years. Carl had rejected the move they made to Bloomsburg, complaining he was too far away from his buddies in the 4 x 4 club he had joined. Every chance he got, was spent with his buddies. And sadly, the four-wheel drive truck became his mistress. At least that is the reason she believed was the reason for the lack of intimacy. Kathy lost her ability to walk for three years. Having to rely on a wheelchair and an attendant for her daily needs. Carl surely wasn't going anywhere with the pretty attendant girls coming daily. Roommates just don't do that. For years, she attended church in her wheelchair with Carl by her side. At that time, Carl stayed by her side kept her head steady while she drank the wine (grape juice), and ate the bread. One of the worst couples counseling sessions during their marriage was Carl's affirmation for being asexual. (He doesn't want to hurt you.?! #%&+). Having your Pastor talk to you about your sex life, and fail to support sex as the Bible encourages; shows such hypocrisy, Kathy made that her last day. She remained a Christian and morally correct, but organized religion wasn't her preference.

"I heard that. I was married for thirteen years before she made me move out. I was out working on a job and came home to divorce papers. Apparently, she found herself someone who worked with her and didn't travel." This was true and Deuce hated to admit it. *Familiarity is good,* he thought.

"Carl was his name. He adopted my son when he was six, but refused to deal with him as he grew up. Hell, all he wanted to do was hang with his buddies," Kathy recalled.

"Just forget him Kathy, he's an asshole. How he could walk out the day after Jeff came home just floors me," Shari added.

Just then, John walked up behind Shari and kissed her on the neck. "Been waiting long?"

Having started on the second rum and Coke, Shari turned around on her stool and replied, "We just got here. Want a drink?"

Deuce, leaning on the bar in front of Kathy, stood tall and extended his hand to John. "How you doing. Name is Deuce." He said in his southern drawl.

John, a thin, balding, thirtysomething, reached and shook his hand. "John," he replied. "What you drinkin', John?" He asked.

Without hesitation, "Captain and Coke." John had just gotten his check but still hadn't gotten it cashed. He would welcome the drink.

"New! Captain and coke for John here." The hundred-dollar bill still laid on the bar. "And give yourself a ten-dollar tip while you're at it."

"Just here to pick up the wife." He teased. As he leaned in for a *this is my woman kiss.*

"If I let him," Shari retorted.

"That's what I was hoping with her cousin." Deuce smiled at Kathy, who felt his glare. "That's my plan anyway."

It's about time you got out Kathy," John told Kathy. "Time, you let your hair down and have some fun. How did Shari talk you into it?"

"Well, she needed the ride, and you need insurance. Two birds with one stone."

"I figured as much," he said with a smile. "You know you have our business… Babe?" John turned caressing Shari's hand. "Can I have a minute of your time."

When John's drink arrived, Shari grabbed him by the arm with one hand and her rum and Coke in the other. Then the couple moved to a nearby table to be alone. Deuce and Mike were now surrounding Kathy. Mike sat on the stool he had given up earlier, while Deuce remained on her right. Kathy was surprised to see Mike was still there.

"Kathy, right?" Mike commented as he took a drink of his Budweiser. "What the hell are you doing in a place like this?"

"Well, actually, I live nearer to this place than you. I should ask you the same question, but I know you're working in the area. "You from West Virginia too?" Kathy looked at the blonde in the cowboy hat wondering how much of a player he really was. Here is a gorgeous guy with a great body, who travels for his job. Chances are he has had numerous affairs wherever he went. Was he looking to score again? *Wrong tree!* she consciously thought, but unconsciously she could fantasize Alan Jackson.'"

"My home is in Ripley. I get home, maybe three times a year; depends on the work." Mike turned towards Kathy as he talked. His blue eyes were soft and filled with beautiful eyelashes.

"Yep, we're both from West Virginia. Now Huey over there is from Ohio. We are from all over, but we all belong to the same Union. I help Mike there. He's the welder and I hand him the rods. I'm a welder's helper," added Deuce.

"As for this guy, don't let him fool you. He'll do about any job there. He is just waitin' for retirement. He's working as many hours as needed, at the simplest jobs. The question is, what are you doing here with this old man anyways?" Mike was just fishing.

This blonde is every woman's fantasy. Blonde, blue eyes, great body, and a blonde mustache. Hell, he's an Alan Jackson's the fantasy come true. Why in the hell is he talking to me? Is it because I'm talking to Deuce? Kathy took the moment to dream.

Kathy, leaned back away from Mike. "What the hell are you talking about?" Looking at Mike and taking offense, "This is the first time in a long time I've been to this bar, never met you folks, and never planned to. Only came here to help my cousin retrieve her husband from work. As soon as I'm finished, we're heading back to the Lake."

"What lake?" Deuce interjected.

It's a lake not too far from here. "Kathy replied, deliberately withholding the name.

"Beaver Lake?" Deuce asked. Deuce knew this lake. Prior to taking this job, he had checked into staying at the Lodge. *How could I be so lucky.*

"Yeah, Shari and John have a house, that overhangs the Lake."

"That's where I stay, at the Lodge." Deuce couldn't believe his luck. "I got in on Monday and asked for the closest motel here. New here, gave me the directions to the Lodge." Deuce was amazed. *She's the one. Now, I'm sure.*

"That's cool. I... We grew up there. My great-grandfather had owned it at one time and I have family still living there." Kathy was proud to know her great grand-father had owned it at one time. From that time, she, Kathy knew that Lake as hers. She swam, picnicked, ice skated, sledded, fished, and fell in love, at the Lake.

"Deuce, do they have any more rooms there? It's twenty miles to my hotel. I wouldn't mind checking it out. What do you pay for a week?" Mike inquired. He looked at Kathy as he talked.

Deuce saw what Mike was doing. He wanted to move in on Kathy. And that was not going to happen, "Nope. You're out of luck. She's booked. There might be a room next week, the Little League World Series is happening, so I need to find another room somewhere else." Deuce hoped that would discourage him from even inquiring anymore.

He knew Mike. If he got a chance he would scoop Kathy up, fuck her up, and never look back. In his opinion, Mike was a male slut.

"How do you like it at the lake?" Kathy asked Deuce.

"It's beautiful, but they need to do something about those lily pads. They are way out of hand." Deuce took another drink from his beer and it was empty. "New! We need another round here!"

"Not for me, I've got to get home. Besides, I'm driving. John wants another before we go, but I'm sure he needs to get home to clean up and eat. He's been at work all day and it's been hot. And I don't blame him." Kathy was nearly done with her second beer, and she was ready to leave.

"Come on, you're the best-looking thing in this joint. You leave and I won't have any reason to stay. I'd have to look at Deuce's ugly mug," Mike complained. "I have to look at too many ugly mugs all day. Hell. I came here to see some beautiful ladies, and the best-looking one is leaving. Damn!"

Kathy didn't truly believe him, but it felt good to hear. Especially from a gorgeous blonde. She had been starved of compliments for a long time, Carl never told her she was beautiful, or even anything that resembles a compliment during most of her marriage. This type of neglect set her up to be a target for those who prey on needy women with low self-esteem. Here she was, a sitting target.

"Give me a minute and I'll check with Shari." Kathy turned with a bump into Mike's legs. She noted how muscular they were even through his work pants. To her It felt great to be admired, for whatever the reason.

Kathy walked through the crowd of pipeliners, who seemed to come out of nowhere and surround the table. Although it was a short distance to the table, her movement through the crowd attracted the attention of love starved men. Kathy felt hot stares directed her way. The noise grew, as did the stench of sweat from hard work. Shari saw her coming and automatically drank down the last of her rum and Coke.

"Are you done drinking with the men now?" Shari asked, knowing, Kathy rarely drinks. "Who was that blonde sitting with you? He's gorgeous."

"Mike, remember? He's working on the pipeline with Deuce. He's from West Virginia, just like Deuce."

"Deuce is a pretty nice guy, though. How long are you going to be here?" Shari wondered.

"I don't know. I do know Deuce is staying at the Lodge until he has to get out for the Little League World Series. That's the end of August. He asked if you guys wanted to go to the Lodge for a drink, after John gets cleaned up. What should I tell him?" Kathy left the decision up to Shari and John. She was not going alone, and if they said they didn't want to go, it was fine with her.

"Listen, I have beer at the house and haven't gotten my check cashed yet. Why don't we invite him up to the house? "John wanted to repay Deuce for the drink. He also hated to borrow or owe.

"You're going to have to invite him. John, I don't want to give him the wrong impression. I'm not ready to start a relationship." Kathy loved to flirt for drinks and attention. But the ache still permeated her soul.

Over a month ago, he walked out, one day after Jeff came home. She wasn't ready for any type of relationship, especially with a pipeliner. *In fact*, she thought, *they probably have AIDS*!

John didn't hesitate. He popped out of his seat and sprinted directly to Deuce. "Deuce, I heard you're staying at the Lodge. After you get cleaned up, why don't you come down to the house and have something to eat? I've got the beer."

Walking up behind John came Kathy." Mike, you're welcome to come along too." Kathy was fairly sure he wouldn't come. Like her mom taught her, it's polite to ask.

"Deuce?" Mike asked "you want?

"Kathy, you coming?" Deuce asked. "I haven't had home cooking in a long time. I been all over the past month and this is first time."

"I'm ready now." Turning to Kathy, "You?" he looked like a puppy with a bone. There was no getting out of it.

"Let's roll! I can't get changed since I didn't bring clothes, but I'm sure you guys don't mind." Kathy looked at Mike, then Deuce doing a slight nod of yes and a smile that needed coaxed by a yes.

"You'd look good in anything you wore." Deuce remarked slyly.

"Hell, she'd look good wearing nothing!" Mike quickly interjected with a wink Kathy's way.

That proved it! SLUT!" She'd met his kind before, despite his addicting looks. *He's looking in the wrong place for a piece of ass!* Never one to sleep around, Kathy still liked eye candy.

Even with a lack of sex with Carl, she never strayed. She mostly just became used to it. Anyway, Carl degraded her when she approached him. The one common phrase she will never forget was, *you should've married a stud*. This was to discourage her from expecting sex very often. Maybe once a month if she was lucky, for over twelve years. It tore at her self-esteem. Even when she wore Victoria Secret, it was only sleeping apparel. Over and over, Kathy tried to talk to Carl about her needs, only to be degraded or ignored. By this time, sex became unnecessary.

"Ready to go?" Kathy asked.

"Well are you guys coming too?" Shari pleaded. "Mike? You can use our shower if you want."

Her excitement was palpable. "I got some corn on the cob and some fried chicken waiting for us. I even have a case of Bud light."

"That's the best offer I got all day!" Mike replied.

"Kathy you're staying too, aren't you? It's the least we can do for helping us out." Shari was hopeful Kathy would stay too.

"Well, I suppose. I still need to do a presentation, so while you're cooking, I'll just jabber it off to you. Okay?" Kathy needed to get this last presentation done.

"Entertainment while I cook. Sounds good to me." Shari replied.

Kathy didn't care if she showed the presentation or not. She was starving. No time for lunch today. And with an empty stomach, her head was buzzing from two beers. But she sure did enjoy the company.

"What presentation?" Asked Mike wondering what the hell she was talking about.

"I'm an Insurance Agent. I was going to show them affordable life insurance."

"Oh, I've got plenty of that." Mike said cockily.

"Well, I'm willin' to listen. I may not need it, but you can present it to me anytime." Deuce was willing to do whatever it took. *This one's not getting way that easy,* he thought. "Let me finish my beer, pay New, get cleaned up, and I will be there directly."

"Deuce, we are the last house on the east side of the Lake." John extended his hand. When Deuce heartily grabbed his hand, John realized his strength. He associated that with his pipeline job.

"We'll see you all later?" Shari needed a definite count for dinner.

"We're comin'!" Mike reacted like he had won the lottery.

Deuce heard one thing, but he had other ideas. Mike wasn't going to make it. He was sure of it.

Although Mike never knew about Deuce's propensity to follow a schedule, no one could stop him now. This was the third year since his family died by an arson fire. His mom and dad never had a chance. Family feuds in West Virginia took a toll on his family.

Heading for the door, Kathy paused to wait for Deuce, so she could see which car was his. She watched as he paid New, adding a twenty-dollar tip. This was on top of the many tips she received from him earlier. She became overwhelmed, hugging Deuce. With that, Deuce opened the door for Kathy and walked her to her car.

Deuce reached to open her door, "Aren't you a gentleman!" Kathy, smiled like a teenage girl. She hadn't felt this way in forever. The last time was with Carl at the beginning of their relationship. Kathy quickly dipped into the car, "See you there." Nervously she cranked the engine.

John and Shari were already waiting in the backseat. With the windows down, they smiled as Deuce said his final goodbyes "BE CAREFUL!" was all he said as he walked around the building to his car.

Chapter 3

Let the Games Begin

Once in the car, John yelled, "Who the hell were those guys anyway?"

"Now you ask! You're the one who invited them to dinner and you ask that? Just someone Kathy got free drinks from." Shari smiled at Kathy's courage. In her younger years, she had the same audacity, but after four children and weight gain came, she lost her confidence, what little she had.

"John! Just chill. I went in there for a purpose. I saw the Harley outside so I thought I could find the guy that rode it and charm my way in. I got a free drink, or was it two. I figured I could find the guy that rode it by looking for guys in skullcaps, with Harley tattoos, or Harley emblems. I saw Deuce. Before you came in he was wearing a Confederate skullcap. I asked, but he didn't own a Harley. He bought drinks for us though, didn't he?" Kathy interjected.

"Who was the cowboy?" John asked suspiciously.

"He works with Deuce. They both work for the pipeline going through the state. They both came from West Virginia, and they will probably be working in the same area until sometime after the Little League World Series. I guess Deuce is the only one staying at the Lodge. Mike is staying somewhere else." Kathy reassured John, there was no other reason. "That Mike is a player. Probably has a girl in every city. So, there would never be anything between him and me. He can play somewhere else. But he's still welcome for dinner, I'm sure. Hell, he's good eye candy." Kathy left it at that. She decided to concentrate on driving. *It's a nice dream. But I know better.* Five more miles to go.

"What do you think about Deuce?" Shari probed. "He seemed like a nice guy. Did you see his eyes? Kind of sparkly, weren't they? He seems really nice." She repeated that point three times. Her "mommy" tone came out. Or maybe grandma was being channeled through her.

"Yeah, I don't know. He's kind of cute. He has money. I love his accent. Those eyes are gorgeous. I doubt he's a player," Kathy replied.

Shari wanted her cousin to be happy. She knew with the M.S. In remission, and being free of Carl, Kathy could find someone who could love her the way she deserved. Even though it's only been over a month since Carl walked out, she knew it had been years since she'd been loved.

"Shari, just let it go. Fuck men!" Kathy spouted.

"Now that's the spirit! Certainly, can't hurt. But, of course, you're a virgin again after all this time. You didn't come to get back on the horse or they say "back in the saddle again"." Shari replied.

Kathy turned up the radio to drown Shari out. Country music had good and bad songs. The good songs made her forget, the bad ones, made her remember. It was always a tossup. *"Ten Thousand Angels,"* was the song playing. It was one of those in between songs.

The lake appeared quickly. It was a sanctuary in and of itself. Kathy reminisced as she drove past the Lodge, the closed down pool, her grandmother's house, and her great grandmother's house. The memories of family reunions, picnics, and ice skating made her miss her grandparents. Shari had lived with her grandparents, most of her growing years. Kathy never understood why for the longest time, but enjoyed the summers picking blueberries, strawberries, huckleberries, and raspberries with Shari. Our grandmother made cakes, custards, breads, and shortcakes from all they brought home. Now, all that was left were memories. Our grandmother died in 1995, followed by our grandfather, five years later. Her aunt June, Shari's mother, bought the house to keep it in the family after her father died.

Shari and John's house appeared quickly. It was an older home, with its own charm. Sitting on the edge of the water, with a porch made from mountain stone, extending over the water. It was where they sat most evenings listening to the bullfrogs call for their mates.

The parking area's two parking spots were blocked. "What's the matter with the car?" Kathy inquired as she pulled her car into a grassy area near the porch.

"Transmission is fucked up," John said with a frustrated sigh. "Damn thing! Fuckin' gonna cost $500 to fix it. I could probably fix it if I had the parts, but then I don't have the time. You know, I'm starting a weekend job."

"No, what are you doing?" It was news to her.

"I'm delivering papers. I know it's stupid, but it will give us a little extra cash. Well, it would if we didn't have to pay for a transmission." John spoke with his head hanging low.

"Where do you deliver? Is it close?" Kathy wondered how he was doing it without a car.

"I deliver around the lake and up the hill behind Grandma Sones' house. I usually drove and it would take me an hour. Now it takes two hours and a half. I try to do the hill first. The fuckin thing kills me. Thank God it's not winter and I do it early in the morning."

The threesome crawled from the car and made their way up the steps to top of the porch. From there they could see the north end of the lake and the trees on the point, just in front of the Lodge. The trees hid the Lodge, but you could see the dock, packed with boats, both fishing and speed boats. In the middle of the Lake, row boats with fishermen were tossing their lines. Amazing, even with the all the Lily pads, a man in a boat reeled in the fish he caught with ease.

"Kathy, do you want a beer before we eat?" Shari asked as she opened the door.

"To tell you the truth, I need to get something in my stomach. I haven't eaten since this morning and I really feel the two drinks I had at the Inn." Kathy knew it wasn't smart to drink on an empty stomach, but she figured she'd grab something eventually.

"You want a sandwich now?" Shari offered. "The chicken will take a while, and I need to husk the corn."

"Sounds good." Kathy didn't want to sit and do nothing. The busier she was the less time she had to mull over her past.

"Is ham salad okay?" Shari talked as she walked towards the kitchen. The house was void of children. Her three surviving children barely made their presence known until their curfew. Usually around nine o'clock in the evening they started to trickle in.

Things had been morose since Anna, the oldest died in a house fire. Shari blamed herself. Anna had been rebellious all her life. Shari knew she was doing drugs, but had no control over that. One evening, while her boyfriend was out of town scoring some drugs, she was awakened by the fire, overcome by smoke, and died. Although it was classified as an accident, Shari and John firmly believed it was arson. Kathy had vivid memories of the loss as she was the one who drove 24 hours straight to help Shari bring her ashes home. It was very memorable!

Instead of allowing Shari to make her a sandwich, Kathy followed her to the kitchen and snatched the ham salad and bread to make her own. After concocting the sandwich, she went to the porch.

"I still need the corn husked!" Shari exclaimed.

"Where is it? I'll get it. You have your hands full with the chicken. Just point the way."

"On the mud porch." Shari pointed the way.

"Why do they call it that? Mud porch. Anyways?" Kathy asked.

"Well, mines muddy." Shari replied with a grin.

Kathy located the corn on a white metal table filled with other food items. The corn was in a white plastic Thank You bag. "Where did you get the corn?", Kathy asked, walking by the woman with the flour covered hands.

"Down at Styers' farm. I think this is butter and sugar, but there may be yellow corn mixed in." If they had had Silver Queen, Id' had gotten that, but apparently, I was too late."

Finding a chair facing the driveway, Kathy waited for Deuce and Mike to arrive. John had immediately gone for a shower. He never hesitated.

Kathy placed the bag of corn on the ground and grabbed her first ear, hoping the sandwich would soothe her indigestion. *Not only should you eat before the second drink; you should always* **have** *Tylenol with you,* Kathy thought.

Husking corn was such a common activity, but she forgot a plate to place the corn on. "*Damn*! There's the other reason to eat!" Kathy set the ear back down on the bag and stood to go for a plate, when she saw Shari approaching with one in her hand.

"Forget something?" Shari asked with a smile."

"Damn alcohol," Kathy laughed. "Is the chicken ready to go on the grill?"

"Not yet. I thought I'd wait until John was out of the shower. Besides I want to give Deuce and Mike enough time to get here."

"You really think they'll show up?" Kathy asked anxiously.

"By the way they were hitting on you, I'd be surprised if they didn't show!" Shari replied.

"Well grab an ear, and we'll get this done," Kathy grabbed the ear she had dropped, while Shari grabbed another. As they husked the corn, John came out through the door carrying a can of beer.

Kathy, are you ready for a beer?" He asked.

"Not yet, but I'll let you know."

"Hey, what about me?" Shari protested.

"You're busy," John teased. "I figured you would be needing your hands to cook. You can't be holding a beer and cook."

"You ASS! Get me a beer!" she commanded.

Soon John returned with a beer for Shari as she dove into the corn, grabbing two ears at once. They all were sitting quietly, listening to the rustling leaves, a dog barking in the distance, the cars driving on the road across the lake, and the sound of corn being husked. It had been about an hour since they left the Inn. Still, it was just the three of them. John had two more beers, while Kathy got herself a can of Coke.

"How long do we have to wait anyway," Kathy asked "I'm famished. Well, maybe not famished, but hungry."

Shari got up and started walking towards the door. "Me too. I'm going to get the chicken started. John, can you get the corn started? The kettle is on the back porch."

"Why don't I cooked the corn on the grill? I'll get the grill started." John got up and walked to his gas grill. He had recently purchased it from a yard sale, and after he had cleaned it up, it worked like a charm. This was the first time he did corn on the grill; yet he wrapped it like a pro. He had the corn cooking in no time, then resumed his position on the porch with his beer.

"How you been doing Kathy?" John asked. "Is Jeff working?"

"Yeah, he is working for Ames Department store. The problem is, we just found out the store is closing in the next two months. He put applications in at the mall, hopefully something will come of it. But he has so much anger, another reason that Carl walked out on us, and that kind of scares me," Kathy replied. "I don't know what to do. But with him working and my job, I don't see him often."

John didn't know what to say, but he got his answer. "Have you started dating again?"

"No, it hasn't been that long since Carl left. I know it's over, but it's not easy moving on.

"You don't have to commit, just have fun!" John quipped slyly.

"Easy for you to say." Kathy was not sure how to do that. The idea of: *just have fun,* implied sleeping around. *Why do men think it's so easy to move on?*

Again, the Lake sounds filled the air. The sun's heat began to fade into warmth. The sounds of the cars across the lake grew louder and suddenly it became obvious that a car was approaching. Kathy's stomach began to knot. *A white Cavalier, one silhouette, which one?* The driver looked for the best area to park, which was in the driveway, behind Kathy's car. For a moment, there was no movement as if the driver was still deciding whether to get out.

John rose to his feet as the car parked, attempting to see who accepted his offer. As the door opened, "Hey Deuce, come on up!"

"Gotta get a beer. Be right up!" he said pulling a six pack of Bud Lite from the back seat.

"Where's Mike?" John asked.

"He had a go to Williamsport to change, so he decided not to come over this time. He said he might be around tomorrow, but I gather he has gotten some other things on his mind." Deuce gave John a sly *you know*. What he didn't tell him was that he had told Mike to find something else to do. He didn't want competition. "Where's the little lady? Deuce asked, meaning Shari.

"Cooking, It's the best place for her." John took a large manly gulp of beer just as Shari walked out through the propped open door.

"Best place for me, eh?" Shari bulked. "And the best place for you is at work. Would that be a fair assessment?"

"You go girl!" Kathy jumped in.

"Now, don't be startin' cause I'm here, just to make me feel at home." Deuce joked. "That's why I'm not back there." He Looked at Kathy and winked. "Now where do you want this?" He asked referring to the beer.

"I'll take that," Shari said. "Since it's the best place for me, I'll take it to the kitchen fridge while I keep cooking."

"Kathy, do ya want one?" Deuce ask as he walked to the chair beside her, noticing she was drinking soda.

"Why not!" she said as he handed her one, ready or not.

Deuce sat down beside Kathy as she began her evaluation. One of her ways was to sit back and let them talk. By observing, listening, and allowing them to hang themselves, Kathy felt that was the way to weed out the assholes. Little did she know how wrong she was.

"Deuce, where are you working? You're with the pipeline, right?" John asked.

"We're workin' outside of Benton right now. Soon we'll join up with the pipeline going towards Williamsport, which joins the next leg of the pipeline." Deuce reciprocated, "where do you work?"

"Bardo's Cement Company. It's right there in town. How long have you been working on the pipeline?"

"Been there since mid-June. But, workin' on the pipeline for nearly thirty years. It's a family thing. Dad worked the pipeline so it seemed the right thing to do. Figured at the time it was the best paying job, and I already knew how to weld. Hell, her brothers are all in it too. But I'm the oldest and I get to retire first." Deuce turned and smiled at Kathy. "How long have you been selling insurance sweetheart?" Kathy never liked being called sweetheart by those who did not know her. But Deuce's drawl changed that. His baritone voice reminded her of one of her favorite actors, Sam Elliot. The mustache did not hurt either. And, there were those eyes. "I just started there a month ago."

"You are pretty, that's for sure. Of course, I always did have a thing for redheads," he commented as he smiled a wily smile. "How do you like it? The job that is." **Commented [CS1]:**

"Smart ass!" Kathy retorted wondering why guys must always reply like that. "I like it. It's not easy, but overall, it's pretty good; the job that is."

Deuce liked this one better than the rest. She had spunk. "Good to know she likes her job. The job I'm on, some of the guys don't give a fuck about safety. I have fun with the foremen when they tell me to do somethin' I know damn well ain't right. They tried to run me off many times, but all I'd have to do is call the great white father in Tulsa, and he'd straighten them out. Like Granny Rose use to say, what's right is right, what's wrong is wrong." Deuce had a serious look when he spoke those words. The truth was, his own brother was disabled due to safety violations.

"I hate that," John jumped in. "It was the same way where I work. Some of those foremen don't know their ass from a hole in the ground."

Kathy watched as the men began to converse, comparing job related accidents. "*Testosterone,*" she thought. Still, she couldn't stop watching Deuce as he told the stories of the dangerous jobs he had and the countries he worked in. Sweden, Germany, and Italy to name a few. She was intrigued. The furthest away she ever got from her hometown was Texas for a short time, so the stories he told charmed her. Shari, busy making dinner, walking back and forth delivering the beer, occasionally paused to listen to Deuce's story.

"John, did you check the corn lately?" Shari asked. "The chicken's done," Shari stood over the grill.

"Shit!" John cried out as he jumped to his feet and ran to the grill. The aluminum had gotten black on the side facing the fire. "Corn's done!" he called. He placed the wrapped corn on a plate gingerly with his fingers. "This is a serve yourself meal. I'm leaving these here," and he placed them on a small table.

"Isn't that the way it's supposed to be? It's the only way I know. Deuce, glaring at Kathy, "ain't that right, little lady"

"Yep, buffet style." Kathy added.

"That's right." Deuce stood and held his hand out to Kathy, "ma'am?" Kathy gladly accepted and placed her hand in his. *This is a first*

"yes". Three more to go. Deuce thought.

"Thank you, sir," Kathy responded as she so welcomed the gesture. She couldn't remember the last time she met a man like him. *In fact, she didn't think she ever had,* she thought.

Shari walked from the house with a large bowl full of potato salad. She placed it on the table with the corn. John had also placed the chicken on the table. "Does anyone need another beer?" asked Shari.

"Sure do ma'am" said Deuce as he tipped the ball cap which replaced his skullcap. His skullcaps and dew rags were mostly worn for work. He had begun to wear them when he was in Vietnam, and depended on them to chase the sweat from his brows.

"Get me one too!" interjected John.

"You Kathy?" asked Shari.

Kathy wasn't even paying attention. She was standing there, just staring at Deuce, wondering what he must have looked like as a young man. In her mind's eye, she saw a man with auburn hair, blue eyes, and mustache to match his hair, strong chest, legs, and arms. He was a hard worker, and now with years spent in the sun, his face possessed well-defined lines. Kathy imagined all the places and events that helped form those lines.

"Kathy, Kathy, Kathy!" Shari explained.

Kathy wasn't even paying attention. She was just standing there staring at Deuce. "Yes." She answered without knowing the question, but hoped it was correct. She was suddenly jolted out of her fantasy world and hoped no one noticed.

"Will do. Three beers, John, you get the beer and I'll get everything else." Shari grabbed John by the arm and they walked in the house, leaving Kathy and Deuce to themselves. Shari saw Kathy staring at Deuce, knowing she had just covered for her.

"Where do you live?" Deuce inquired as he picked up a chicken leg off the plate and took a bite. His mustache caught everything that fell.

Kathy, again enthralled by Deuce, caught herself quickly, "Oh, about thirty miles from here," she replied evasively.

"Williamsport?" He said still chewing his food. She heard, 'Wimensput.'

"What?" She said with bewilderment.

Deuce swallowed. "Williamsport."

"No," She said. "Bloomsburg." Kathy hated to give him that much information, but Bloomsburg's a large town.

"Been there," he said as he took another bite. He watched as Kathy maneuvered around him. She tried to get at the chicken, brushing his stomach as she passed, and an urge he had been missing shot to life again. His heart started pounding so hard, he was afraid she would hear, as she passed by again. He noticed sweat running down the side of his face, He'd have to put his dew rag back on. This was the other reason he depended on the dew rag. *I'm gonna have this one. I feel it.* He thought.

"Where do you call home?" Kathy asked, drawing the attention back on him.

"A little town called Clendenin. You might've heard of it. Paul Harvey talked about it once. It's about twenty miles north of Charleston on Route 119. I have a farm there with three hundred acres and a couple of gas wells on it. I don't farm right now, but I plan on it when I retire."

"When's that?" Kathy asked in between bites, thankful for his long answers. She had been famished.

"Well, officially next year, but that's not definite. I might stick it out for a couple more years, that's if they don't piss me off!"

John and Shari arrived with the beer, paper plates, and utensils. John handed Deuce his beer first. "Didn't mean to desert you like that, but my wife got a little sick," John explained apologetically.

"This is my last one." Kathy said as she accepted the beer John handed her. "I think I've drunk a six pack, or is it drank? Shit, maybe I shouldn't even have this one!"

"You're right the first time. Of course, you're talking to a hillbilly, through and through." Deuce smirked.

"You wouldn't believe I'm an elementary school teacher, would you? Kathy admitted. "But damn. I couldn't find a full-time position. It's all politics. It's who you know or who you blow."

"Really? My auntie Carla is on the Kanawha County school board." Deuce offered, "they are always looking for teachers." *Might be easier than I thought*! Deuce realized.

There was silence, as they all began to partake in the food. Deuce, glad to have homemade potato salad again, piled a glob on his plate. Kathy turned her sights to the corn-on-the-cob. Shari and John helped themselves to the chicken, and they all sat with their beers, enjoying the sounds around the Lake.

The warm air of the day cooled and the bullfrogs began their baritone calls to their mates. Fireflies intermittently dotted the darkness of the lawn. The crescent moon hung above the far mountain, amidst a few clouds. The calm was as intoxicating as the beer. One by one, each of Shari's and John's children returned home for the night.

"Shari," Kathy said breaking the silence. "You mind if I stay the night? I think I had too much to drink. Do you have something I could wear to bed?" Having had so much alcohol, Kathy knew this was the smart thing to do.

"You know, Kathy you can take Dustin's bed; he can sleep on the couch. That's his favorite place to sleep anyways." Shari thought that was the best solution.

"I need to call home and let Jeff know I'll be home in the morning. Kathy knew Jeff would be perturbed if she didn't call. With his A.D.H.D., he got very agitated very quickly.

Deuce, sitting quietly as the two spoke, was glad to be there. Kathy was staying at the Lake for the night. *I've got to get her back here tomorrow night. I need the chance to talk to her alone.* He glanced around for a path into the woods. None. He then got an idea. *She's got a Saturn. I'm going to get her to show it to me.*

"Kathy! You got a Saturn. How do you like it?" Deuce asked.

"I love it!" And she did. She was proud of it, mainly because she was the first to ever own it. The miles on that car were hers.

"Is that a twin cam?" Deuce inquired.

"Yeah, what does that mean anyway?"

"I'm no mechanic, but I think it helps burn the fuel" Deuce admitted. "But I sure would like to see what it can do."

"What you mean? How fast it can go? I don't think so." Kathy was hesitant. *Where was this going?*

"No! That's not what I was thinking." He had to save this one. "They are supposed to shift smoother." *Good save*! He thought. "Want to take a ride around the Lake? I've heard some bragging on em. I want to see it if he was bullshittin' me."

Kathy's chest tightened. Deuce seemed nice, as she had been enjoying his stories, but her anxiety just peaked. "Wait a minute, I better go the bathroom, and then we'll go."

"Granny Rose used to say, in one door, out the other." Deuce reiterated.

"Shari, I need help finding something. Let these guys hang, and help me out, please." Kathy needed to get her opinion. Kathy, grabbed her by the shoulders, and as soon as they got out of sight, "Should I?"

"What? Should you do what?" Shari was confused because she wasn't paying attention.

"Deuce wants me to give him a ride around the Lake."

"AND? What's wrong with that? Are you surprised? He wants you girl!" She giggled. "You're free. Oops, you're not for sale or anything. Isn't that funny? Like, you're going to sell him anything anyway." Shari drunkenly rambled and laughed.

"You're no help! I'm going, but if I don't come back, you know where he lives, and you know where he works. Right?" Kathy slurred just a little. In her opinion she could drive, *And I'm only going to the Lodge and back,* she thought.

"Kathy, did you know you're nuts? He won't do anything. And if he did, John would take care of him. So, shut up and go." Shari turned and walked away.

Kathy felt a twinge that consoled her. Her radar was beeping. She wasn't sure why, but she was feeling it. She waited in the dining room for just a few more minutes. *I hope I'm not tempting fate, ignoring my intuition, but it's never been very good anyways.* Kathy decided she was over analyzing again.

She walked back to the group, where Kathy noticed Deuce was gone. "What happened to the man that was just here?" She asked. Shari was sitting on John's lap by now, looked up and pointed towards the back of the porch. Back in the corner, deuce stood in a stance only a man could stand in.

"You were in the bathroom and he had to… you see." Shari slapped her head back down on John's shoulder.

"YOU READY?" Kathy called to Deuce.

Deuce finished, pulled the front of his jeans around under his belly. His *ass was small and tight. His legs looked tight. His arms looked strong in proportion to his stomach. Apparently, he's been drinking for a long time, so much for him."*

"You gonna let me drive?" Deuce assumed.

"No, I'm not. You can drink," Kathy said, exaggerating how inebriated he was by stressing that, "you're slurring just a little."

"Look who's talking." He grinned.

"Wasn't that a movie?" Kathy just loves come backs. "At least I'm the one insured, and I'm the one who grew up here, so I know the roads. Enough said."

"Aren't you frisky. Bet you've got a temper," Deuce said just under his breath.

"You want to know?" She asked hearing his comment. "If necessary. I do," Kathy whispered as he passed her on the steps, brushing her firmly on the way to the car. She noticed the sweat running down the side of his face.

This is going to be fun, but it looks like I'll have to stay one step ahead.

Chapter 4

The Slow Seduction.

Kathy, was near the bottom of the steps before she remembered his car was parked behind her. "Okay, you'll have to move your car if you want to ride in mine." She told Deuce.

"Not a problem. I have to get another pack of cigarettes anyway." He was headed to the car as he turned and said, "Would you rather I drove?" knowing she would say no.

"You've been drinking," she repeated, knowing she had to control the situation. "Maybe next time."

"So, you're saying there is going to be a next time?" Deuce asked. He hoped he knew the answer. *Give me the next yes, girl*, he thought.

"We'll see. Let's just go for a ride, we can talk about it afterwards," she responded. *Slow down buddy,* she thought as he opened the door. The ding from the ignition alarm, reminded her the keys were in it.

He pulled behind John's car, grabbed his cigarettes, and dew rag from the passenger seat, and threw his ball cap on the seat in its place. *From the early sweat, I know I'll need this,* he assured himself. By the time he reached Kathy's car, the engine was running silently, with a country music station softly playing. "You like country music, eh?" He asked as he sat in the passenger seat.

"Yep. Now what do you want me to do for you to feel how well it shifts? she asked.

"Well the first thing is to get out on the hard top. From there, I'll tell you," Deuce said needing control.

Kathy, did as he said, and stopped. "Now what?"

"Just take me around to the other side of the Lake, and pull into the boat dock. As we go that way, I'll tell you when to accelerate and brake. It will show me how smooth it shifts, compared to mine.

My brother wants me to get rid of my Cavalier, and I might check into getting a Saturn. My uncle has a Saturn and he's been raggin' on me to get one."

Kathy accelerated slowly. The road wasn't quite big enough to do any major acceleration at that spot, but she knew where the road was perfect. "As soon as I get around the first corner in the road, it widens enough for me to push it."

"You da driver!" he exclaimed.

Kathy proceeded, quietly passed the homes along the lake before reaching the curve she was speaking about. As she rounded the curve, she stopped again. "Ready?" she asked Deuce. Not waiting for a response, she shoved her foot to the floor, in the car accelerated for approximately a quarter mile, and decelerated back to a slower speed.

"Whoa! Good pickup on this little thing!" He was seriously impressed. He never realized it was possible for a four-cylinder. Yet, he didn't really care either. The only reason he asked about it was to get Kathy alone. "Let's pull into the boat dock for a minute. I want to check the engine," Deuce said pretending to be interested.

Kathy turned into the dock area and pulled beneath the only streetlight in the lot. It was past the Lodge, which was packed with patrons, yet within a distance she felt safe. With people still pulling into the Lodge and those leaving, she knew she could attract attention if needed. Kathy brought the car to a stop, hesitating for a moment to watch a reflection of the moonlight dancing on the water. Despite the overabundance of Lily pads, or because of them, the Lake had an eerie yet beautiful calm.

Deuce, dragged on his cigarette, and noticed how calm and quiet the lake was. "This is beautiful. I like the way you can see the movement of the water, it's not stagnant."

"It's spring fed. If the Association would take care of the lily pads, it would be less stagnant," Kathy replied, thinking of the time when you could swim from the boat dock to her grandparent's dock. Today, however the lily pads would entangle a swimmer's legs and pull them under. "You believe you could swim over to that little boat house with the light?" Kathy pointed to the light, "the only lily pads back then were in the coves and right along the edges."

"The fish like 'em. They give a good cover, you said you were raised here? Where did your grandparents live?" Deuce wanted know as much as he could.

"You see that light I pointed out? That was my granddads boat house, though it couldn't hold a boat now." Kathy, smiled as she remembered, as a child, going to the boathouse to get a fishing pole and wondering why it didn't have a boat in it.

"You'll have to point it out to me when we go back," Deuce said as he watched her face soften as she spoke of her childhood. "You were close to your grandparents, weren't you?"

"Not as close as I could have been," she replied. "Are we going to look at the engine?" Kathy wanted to redirect the conversation. It still ached knowing how her grandmother died.

"Let's do it!" Deuce said, seeing the sudden change in the conversation. He opened his door first, and swung his feet onto the pavement. "The only thing I don't like is how close it is to the ground."

Climbing out of her side, Kathy reminded him, "your Cavalier isn't much higher."

"But I was debating over a car or a truck for when I retire."

"That's a no-brainer. Get a truck." She said.

"Why?" That response surprised him.

"You'd be able to haul things when you need to."

"Sounds like work to me! And I'm retiring to get away from work. Besides, ya' know, with a truck. someone will be moving." Deuce laughed gently at his own joke.

Deuce stood across the hood smiling at Kathy, and for some reason, he suddenly looked different to her. His smile lines were lit up by the street light, and there was a twinkle reflecting from his glasses. He had put on his dew rag at some point, and looked like the rebel she met earlier. She couldn't figure out which one made him look differently.

Suddenly, *He's cute as hell!* She thought as she watched him walk around to the front of the car.

"You want to pop the hood?" Deuce asked noticing Kathy quietly smiling at him. *Got you preoccupied do I?* As Kathy turned to reach into the window and unlatch the hood, he remarked, "You got what I got, C.R.S., Can't Remember Shit."

"What?" She had no idea what that was.

"C.R.S., Can't Remember Shit. It's going around," he smiled. Deuce lifted the hood and propped it up. The small light lit up the engine compartment. The white Twin Cam was illuminated on the top of the black engine. "Yep, it does make a difference. I like the pickup, and it sure shifts smooth from what I saw."

"But it's too close to the ground," Kathy reiterated.

"Zackly! There is a chance for you yet!" He laughed.

"Chance for what?" Kathy responded smiling at Deuce's boldness.

"You might make it." Deuce said in his deep southern voice.

Kathy felt that sudden twinge in her chest that she felt earlier. 'What?" She wasn't sure why the twinge happened again.

Smiling his best smile, he revealed, "You could make a good hillbilly."

"What are you nuts or something?" She smiled again at his boldness.

He put the hood back down, leaning against the car smoking his cigarette, and while staring at the lake, "So, you grew up here?"

Kathy leaned beside him, "Let's just say I spent lot of time here with my cousin. We used to rule this area! So, we thought."

"So where did you grow up?" He was curious.

"I grew up in Montoursville." Ah, her hometown.

"I work with guys staying in Montoursville. Do you know where the tavern is with the motel?" He asked.

"Yeah, the Wagon Wheel. I know where it is." She remembered Jim again. The only time she had ever seen one of the rooms.

The two fell silent into their own thoughts. *Jim was the first older man I ever dated. He was also from another state.* She remembered it well.

Granny Rose would be glad to see me with a redhead, He thought. *I wonder if she's a real redhead.* In time, I will know.

Deuce reached his arm behind Kathy and leaned closer to her. "Do you know how pretty you are? For a Yankee, that is." He said without looking at her.

"From what I've heard about those West Virginia women, aren't you glad?" She responded, not looking at him either.

"When you approached me at the bar, I thought I was dreamin', until you took the dew rag off my head. You know, you're the first person to take a dew rag off my head without me get pissed off." Deuce turned to Kathy who was looking back, and smiled.

The twinge happened again. She didn't know what to think. *Was that a compliment or a warning*? She froze in consideration. As she did, Deuce leaned towards her and kissed her softly on the lips.

"Thank you, it's been three years since I kissed a beautiful woman," Deuce said as he backed away.

Kathy wasn't entirely surprised by his kiss. She knew he was interested, or he wouldn't have showed up tonight. And his kiss wasn't intrusive, but soft and tender. In fact, she thought, *He's a southern gentleman.*

Kathy leaned in towards Deuce, initiating their next kiss. This time his kiss was deep and passionate. So deep that Kathy had to push him away to get air. "Phew, I guess it has been a while!" she gasped.

Deuce failed to maintain complete control and he knew. *Damn, stand down Sargent*! "Sorry," he was all he could say.

"Let me remind you how it's done." She said as she cupped his face in her hands and pulled him slowly to her lips, giving him soft passionate kisses. Deuce's lips were soft against hers. Their kisses harmonious. Until, Deuce began to become greedy and pushed his way deep into her mouth again. Again, she pushed him away so she could breathe again. "If you want to kiss me, keep that in your mouth. There are only certain times I enjoy it, and this isn't it." Kathy didn't care what she said to him. "I did like kissing you until you shoved you tongue down my throat without notice."

Deuce grabbed her by the waist and pulled her to his lips again. Kathy flinched as he pulled her into his arms and held her firmly. She found herself face to face with him slowly lowering his lips to hers. His lips caressed hers with soft nips. Kathy allowed it to continue. Deuce turned Kathy skillfully and set her on the car in front of him. Her black satin dress made her slide and the kiss was broken.

Kathy came back to reality. Here she was sucking face with some guy she would probably never see again. She thought *Damn he can kiss… Damn he knows how to hold me*. Readjusting, she faced him brushing off the unseen dirt from her dress. "You lied to me. It hasn't been that long since you kissed a woman."

"Maybe so, but she wasn't as pretty as you." Deuce gave her a sly smile and dipped into his pocket for another cigarette. "Seriously, after I had my stroke, a slight one, I have not been with a woman. Good ole Henry hasn't worked. But when you kissed me, Henry woke up. Girl you got it!" He took a long drag from his cigarette, and blew it at Kathy.

"Seriously? You had a stroke?" She asked with concern.

"That's what I said." He retorted.

Kathy was surprised, and yet not. "Deuce, let me have a cigarette." He handed her one and held his Bic up so she could light it. "So, you haven't had sex in… how many years?"

"Three," he lied. It seemed to be the best way to pull women in.

"I thought I had it bad." Kathy remembered her marriage of convenience. "So, 150 times in twelve years wasn't so bad after all."

"What you mean?" Now he was curious.

"Well, I was married twelve years, and I estimate we had sex 150 times. He loved his truck more than me. Or, at least that was the way he made me feel."

Kathy hated remembering the time she begged him to make love to her more often. He made her feel like a freak for wanting it. *"It's part of being married. Intimacy is normal."* She had told him at one point. *"Fuck you!"* Was his normal response as he walked away? *"That's right. That's what I want. I'm not going to stay in this loveless Marriage forever if it doesn't change."* She would yell as he walked away. That was seven months ago. Between then and now, HE elected to move out.

"Oh man, what, was he gay? You are one hot woman. Be glad you're rid of him!" Deuce had hit the jackpot! A love starved woman he would love to feed. "Yeah, if I were him, I wouldn't let you out of my bed, except to eat and go to the bathroom." He smiled, *if you only knew what I wanted to do with you!*

"You know what was funny? When I last talked to his mother, she said she had thought that one of her boys was gay. That floored me. I had never even thought about it that way. I thought he was just a man with issues."

"Issues hell!" Deuce was shocked. "Girl if he wasn't interested in you sexually, he had a hell of a problem. I'd say that boy wasn't hung too tight. He had to be swing'n the other way." Deuce wondered how any man in his right mind could treat a woman like that.

"Well, I wonder why I put up with it as long as I did. You know, I'm glad it's finally over," Kathy said as she leaned into Deuce's arms.

Deuce wrapped his arms around her like a gooey band aid, tightening them to give her just enough room to breathe. He didn't respond verbally, just let out a soft, slow sigh, "I got you now", all while thinking *you're the one.*

Deuce and Kathy spent an hour and a half holding each other. They moved from the hood of the car to the front seat. With steam on the window, and smoke in the car, they found each other. Kathy knew sex in the small car wasn't feasible, especially with this large man. But she welcomed wanting hands caressing her breasts as they kissed. His kiss was in sync with hers.

Deuce grabbed her hand at one point and placed it on his swell. "You woke Henry." As he unbuttoned and unzipped his pants, Kathy noticed he was not wearing underpants. It spooked her.

"Sorry, didn't mean to scare you. Wasn't your husband that big?"

"Oh, he was six foot seven inches big. I'm just not used to seeing a man not wearing underpants under their jeans."

Kathy forgot for a split second, how old Deuce was. Then again, she really didn't know. "You know; I never did ask you how old you are. Not that it matters."

He always liked that, *not that it matters part.* I'm 50. You?"

"I'm 22, twice," she admitted in her own denial way.

"Second time around is always the best." Deuce liked her way. He liked her heart. Mostly he liked her innocence. "But can you cook?" He asked unexpectedly.

"Can I cook? Where did that come from?"

"I haven't found anything that would turn a man away. But maybe that's why he left." He answered cautiously

"Fuck you!" Kathy responded. "I guess you'll never find out."

"So, you think you could cook for me?" Deuce liked her spunk. "Aren't you a spitfire!" He reached to kiss her and she gave herself to him.

Chapter 5

And the Lies Balloon

Kathy refused to stay the night with Deuce at the Lodge and made her way back to Shari's with her hair as mussed as her clothing. Shari was guiltily sitting at the dining room table. There on the floor, lay a stack of newspapers to be delivered. Kathy remembered many mornings wrapping newspapers with her son.

"Don't your boys help?" She asked, as Shari lifted her head to see her standing in the doorway.

"John likes to do it on his own. He says it goes quicker that way," said Shari in a sluggish voice.

"Why aren't you in bed? Worried about me?" Kathy knew she was after what she had said earlier.

"Damn you Kathy, I thought you'd be right back. You let him drive?" Shari asked thinking he took her somewhere. She didn't know where, but she was aware that she had been gone for three and a half hours.

"No, we just parked down at the boat dock and talked." Kathy knew why she was mad.

"Just talked, eh?" Shari asked, sitting up in her chair. "Now, tell me what really happened?"

"Let me get a drink, and I'll tell you. Let's just say, he's well hung." Kathy walked by her into the kitchen. As soon as she opened the refrigerator door and took out a can of sprite, she added, "And he goes commando!"

Shari, couldn't wait for her to return and followed her into the kitchen. "Commando? What's commando?" She had never heard that expression before.

"He doesn't wear underpants!" She said softly as she began to laugh. "He said he stopped wearing them in Vietnam." She continued to giggle, with Shari joining her. "He said he doesn't wear them because… he had the shit scared out of him so often he got use to going without." The two couldn't hold the laughter in any longer.

"Shit scared out of him…ha ha ha…had to change too often…ha ha ha, Are you serious?"

"As serious as a heart attack!" Kathy exclaimed, taking that saying from Deuce. "You know, Deuce is pretty cool. He told me some of the most amazing stories of his time working on the pipeline. You know, he worked on the Alaskan pipeline."

"In Alaska?" Shari asked instinctively.

"Near the Arctic circle at one point. He told me how he and some of his friends got pissed off at his foreman for doing something that put them in danger. So, they lured a grizzly bear into camp and trapped him on the bus with food."

"What the hell was that? What happened?" Shari asked, amazed and afraid at the same time.

"He said he fired a gun to scare it away, and the foreman kissed their ass the rest of the time they were there."

"What else did he tell you?" Shari asked, wondering how crazy this man was.

"Well, he said on one of his jobs, the foreman told him to climb into a ditch that wasn't shored up, and weld a pipe together. He told him, he wasn't going to risk his life, so the foreman got pissed, and fired him. He said he had to put up with his shit for too long, and what's right is right and what's wrong is wrong. So, he threatened to set him on fire and pound the fire out with his acetylene tank." Kathy, smiled when she said that, remembering Deuce's excitement as he told the story.

"You're kidding me!" Shari was shocked.

"That's not all. He left and called The Great White Father in Tulsa, and had his job back the next day. They fired the foreman, though," thinking it was funny Kathy, smiled as she reminisced.

Shari didn't know what to think. "So how did you find out he wasn't wearing underpants?

We couldn't have been talking, you figured that out." Kathy said eluding the question. Kathy's smile told it all. She enjoyed her time with Deuce. He had surprised her with his style. His southern West Virginia style. Oh hell, his Hillbilly style. She was sure. He spoke of the mountain he owned, gas wells on his land, his farm, and his dream of backing up his stream to raise catfish. Seems like a dream to her as she thought about it. *He said you could see for miles from the upper meadow.* Just a dream.

"Shari, I must be nuts. Look at him; he's no looker, but... I like him." She was amazed at herself. "He's funny, and I love his stories."

Shari grinned, seeing Kathy as happy as she was. *It's been a long time since she's been this happy.* Shari was still a little apprehensive. That story about the grizzlies made her wonder, but pounding the fire he had set, out with the tank... Something just wasn't right. "Kathy, are you going to see him again tomorrow? Or, later today? It's one o'clock; did you know that?"

"I told him I had to go home and get some work done, but he asked if I wanted to go eat at Larry's Inn. I said yes. Was that bad?"

"Alone? Just the two of you?" Shari was concerned about her safety. Kathy hadn't been in the dating scene for twelve years. With the stories, Deuce told Kathy, she didn't trust him.

"Yes, alone. Why? Do you and John want to come? I don't think Deuce would mind. And even if he does, fuck 'em." Kathy trusted Shari's instincts to a certain extent, so of course she wanted her to come. Still, she also wanted to talk to him alone. "You still analyzing him? Here's an idea, why don't you and John show up there? That way if things go wrong, you'll be there. I kind of want to be alone with him, yet I'd like you to watch my back. If you know what I'm mean."

"Kathy, you know our car is broken down. How would we be able to get there?" Shari knew Kathy would have to go it alone. She just couldn't invite herself to dinner. Deuce may be able to afford it, but they couldn't. "Besides, you'll have your car, won't you? If he even remotely looks like he's a nutcase, promise you'll leave."

Kathy understood that completely. She was coming from the opposite direction to get to Larry's Inn and Shari and John's access to money was limited. "Listen, if it's okay, I'll come here and stay the night again. That way I can fill you in."

Shari agreed. It seemed like the best solution. Deuce did seem harmless. And, the stories he told Kathy were probably not true. It was hard to see this man as harmful. He had such an enchanting personality.

"Kathy, why don't you and Deuce come over to the Lodge when you're done? In fact, you could eat there too. Then we can walk down and be there when you come in."

"Good idea. I'll be there with or without Deuce. I'm supposed to meet him at six-thirty. We should probably be there for at least an hour if we eat there. So, let's meet at the Lodge around eight, okay?"

Agreeing it was the best solution, Shari and Kathy had finally wound down enough to go to bed. Kathy took a T-shirt from Shari to wear and crawled into Dustin's bed. The night at the Lake was cooler than she had thought it would be, so she pulled the cover up around her shoulders. Her mind pulled her back to the boat dock. She saw Deuce's face, felt his kisses, and wondered why she was so enchanted with him. She fell asleep, with Deuce deep in her memory.

The wide sky was roofed with menacing clouds. She stood watching as a lightning approached. The strikes were larger than normal; the destruction was severe. Kathy looked for shelter. Nothing but trees were offered. In the distance, Deuce stood beneath a dying willow, holding his arms out toward her. She wanted to go to him, something held her back. The Storm approached even faster. She began calling to him for help. He continued to stand there with outstretched arms. Kathy didn't understand why he would let her stand there, knowing she couldn't move. Why wasn't he coming to save her?"

Kathy awoke to the sounds of thunder and flashes of lightening from an early morning thunderstorm. Her dream, still fresh in her mind, had her heart pounding. She sat up, and shook her head. *It was only a dream influenced by the storm,* she thought. *He would never just leave her standing there.* The twinge in her chest happened again. *It just reflects abandonment issues. Thanks Carl,* she thought as she rolled out of bed to empty her bladder. *You messed me up for future relationships. I'll never be able trust anyone again. Of course, maybe that's good.*

Kathy slept restlessly the rest of the night. By daylight, she was ready to leave. Leaving Jeff alone overnight, worried her. Of course, she felt guilty about a lot of things, especially last night. She hadn't kissed a man like that, with that kind of passion, since first meeting Carl. She didn't understand why she was drawn to Deuce. *Was it the attention he showed me? Or was it the need for security?* Kathy didn't know. All she knew was she was going to meet him tonight at Larry's Inn.

Deuce woke with the sun filtering through the window of his room. He slept hard as usual. The beer he had at the Lodge bar, after leaving Kathy, topped with shots of tequila, barely allowed a steady climb of the steps to his room. He hadn't stopped thinking of Kathy however, he wondered if she would show up at Larry's Inn for dinner. *I hope my luck continues,* he thought. *Tonight, she'll be mine.* Deuce patted his pocket, never knowing when he might need it. He always had it with him. "Good ole Granny Rose!"

Chapter 6

The Impending Truth

Taking the day to do paper work for her job, Kathy cleaned the house, and argued with Jeff over her absence the night before. Kathy tried to put last night behind her. Jeff wasn't told about Deuce, and she would let that subject go for another time. Jeff would never want her to see anyone. In his eyes, Carl would be back, even though he had not even called since he walked out two months ago. *Besides, he doesn't have the right to tell me what to do. He's the child, and I'm the parent!* She told herself, knowing she hadn't committed adultery.

The day seemed to drag on. Kathy should have gone grocery shopping, but with her impending date, she couldn't concentrate. Kathy pondered all day on what she should wear. She didn't want to dress sleazy or sexy. She elected Jean shorts and a pink, button-down shirt. Instead of sandals, she wore her white sneakers, and white socks folded down evenly. If she looked like anything; she looked comfortable.

After she dressed, Kathy packed an overnight bag, wondering when to tell Jeff she was spending the night at Shari's again. She would tell him before she dropped him off at work, to avoid any argument. This time she would leave a message on the answering machine. Just like she should have done last night.

Deuce had planned for this for three years. "*So far,*" he thought, "*things are going well. I had my doubts at first, but so far, it's all good.*" He was confident. "*She'll be my third, third, third. The third time, the* third year, and the third girl. It's got to be a record." Deuce loved the way he lured the girls, especially the younger ones.

"Alaska was the thirty-year-old girl; she was the first. She had long black hair and lasted the longest so far. I hope Kathy can top her record." Deuce could only imagine. "With her spunk, I could see it."

Having spent the day at the bar downstairs with his new-found friends, Deuce disappeared to prepare for the evening. He got to know the patrons at the bar, while staying at the Lake but he was hoping his luck would change tonight with Kathy. Deuce grabbed a clean pair of jeans and a black pocketed T-shirt. All his clothing, packed in a worn green duffel bag, reminded him of his time in Germany. Last came the red suspenders.

Deuce's weight fluctuated so often, he thought by buying his jeans two sizes larger and fastening them with suspenders was the way to go. When the suspenders were loose, it showed him; he had lost weight. They were his "bathroom scales."

Five thirty and Kathy was ready. She calculated it would take forty-five minutes from her home to Larry's Inn. She gathered up the last of her make-up and threw it in her overnight bag. She was nervous with teenage butterflies. They make you realize you're doing something new and exciting, or are they telling you there could be danger? She wasn't sure yet, but there was no turning back. She believed it was safe in a familiar bar. Didn't know anyone there, that he didn't know that. She'll have a car, and can and will leave anytime she wants.

During the ride to Larry's Inn, Kathy could only imagine what the night would bring. Either way, it would be her first official date since Carl left. She felt guilty, scared, and excited all at once. Her mind was swimming through each emotion. Kathy decided turn the radio on and up loud. A country song by the Dixie Chicks began with "EARL".

As she listened, she recalled all the wasted years she was married to Carl. "Earl's Gotta Die," turned into "Carl's gotta Die." Kathy sang with full force and found her anxiety was lessened as her empowerment grew. *No one will ever use or abuse me again,* she pledged to herself, *No one will ever neglect me either!*

Larry's Inn showed up on her left too quickly. Butterflies went into overtime. Kathy waited in the front parking lot until she saw the white Cavalier pull in from the opposite direction and followed it to the back of the parking lot. The Cavalier took the first and largest space, while Kathy took the smaller spot further back. When Kathy got out of her car, she was shocked to see his car was as old as it was. Deuce's door squeaked as he opened it to get out. She never guessed it would be in that condition. *With the money, he says he earns, what's with the old car?*

Deuce saw Kathy as soon as her car came in view. He remembered the black dress she wore last night, and wondered what she'd be wearing. It's really didn't matter; he saw all he needed. Her breasts were firm and round with identical erect nipples. He was shocked that she allowed him to pull the spaghetti straps off her shoulders so he could see them, touch them, and even suckle them. It took some coaxing, but he still knew how to do it. *Play on their vanity. They do whatever is needed to prove you wrong.*

Kathy waited at her car, waiting for him to slowly make his way to her. His pace was an I don't care attitude, wait or don't. Kathy waited.

"Hope you're hungry!" Deuce announced. "The food is great. But, not good as Granny Rose's, but damn near. I told New to put us at the table in the back. That way we can talk without yelling over top everyone."

"Oh, I'm hungry. And just to warn you, I won't be eating like a bird." Kathy smiled. She was telling the truth. With everything she had to do today, she forgot to eat. She had snacked on a piece of bologna and drank a pot of coffee. In fact, she planned to get steak, medium rare.

"Dog gone girl! You can eat as much as you want. By the way it looks, you wear it well." Deuce pulled her to him as he caught up to her. "Girl, I've been all over the world and have never met anyone like you." Deuce kissed her deeply, only for a moment, to be sure she would not pull away. That was the last thing he wanted.

She arched her back, feeling his passionate kiss. He had gone in, but learned how deep for how long, last night. As Deuce tried to end the kiss, Kathy initiated her own. She slipped her tongue slow and teasingly into his mouth. He responded, pushing her up on her car hood, pushing his tongue to an overwhelming depth. At that point, she became aware of her surroundings and pushed him away. "Wait... Wait." She felt scared. "WAIT!" Kathy gave him a double shoulder shove with her fists and Deuce took a step back.

"I'm sorry. But, when you kissed me like that, I lost control for a moment. I never had no woman give her tongue like that before." Deuce was shocked. *I see she's ahead of the game. That's one less thing I've got to train her on. The first thing is this pushing me away. That's got to stop.* Deuce was holding his hands up as if a gun was aimed at him. "Have mercy. Promise, I learned my lesson."

Kathy, seeing his child like antics, laughed. "You know, if I ever kiss you like that again, and you go deep sea diving, you will never get to do it again," she warned. Kathy hated to be violated. She wanted to be in control,

"I heard that!" He said, thinking, *when I want it, I'll get it.*

"If you let me have control, when I initiate it, things will go much better." Kathy wanted to make known her position on that subject.

"Girl, I'll give you all the control you want!" Deuce said, knowing what to say.

"Then let's eat," Kathy said, lowering her hand to reach for his.

Deuce took her hand, and softly kissed it. "After you ma'am."

Hand in hand, Kathy and Deuce walked in the front door of the Inn. The Inn was surprisingly crowded. Kathy hoped that meant the food was good, not just the drinks. Finding an empty table in the rear of the establishment, as New suggested, Deuce softly kissed Kathy's cheek, and pulled her chair out for her. But instead of sitting with her, he excused himself to find New.

Within a few minutes, Kathy saw Deuce with New in tow. New had a smile on her face that looked like a child in a candy factory. They made their way through the crowd to the table. New was holding two menus. But without putting them down, she passed by the table giving Kathy a smile. Deuce however, did stop.

"Ma'am, your table is wait'n," Deuce proclaimed as host. He held his hand out to escort her.

"Thank you, sir!" Kathy said, excited to see what else this night would hold. She had never been treated so special, she felt like a Princess.

"New has set us up in the back-dining room," Deuce told Kathy as they walked. "She's a greatly lady." Deuce smiled.

"But you're a great woman!" He knew he had to be sure that Kathy understood where she stood in his eyes.

The two walked into the breakfast area of the Inn, to find a table set up with a taper candle burning in a Bud Light long neck bottle. The lights were dimmed to give a romantic glow. Kathy was taken aback. Her mouth opened to speak, but she had no words in her vocabulary to express how she felt. She just allowed Deuce pull her chair out.

New waited for Deuce to take his seat, and placed the menus in front of them. "Our specials today are; Liver and Onions, Black Diamond Steaks, and Catfish Fillet," she explained, "you know what you want now or should I come back with your drinks first?"

Deuce and Kathy simultaneously said "WAIT!"

"Okay, so what do you want to drink? New smiled as she looked at the two glancing at each other smiling.

"You know what I want. What do you want Kathy?" Deuce asked, "The same as last night?"

"I think I'll have a Pepsi," she said.

"Coke okay?" New questioned.

"Don't you want someth'n in it?" Deuce asked, wondering why she changed to Pepsi.

"Deuce, last night was an exception. I don't usually drink that much, or very often." Kathy retorted.

"Coke it is!" New said as she turned and strutted out the door, towards the bar.

"That's good you don't drink much," Deuce replied. "I don't think I could afford another drinker in the family." Deuce smiled big at Kathy.

"Excuse me? I'm not sure what that meant, but I'm not planning on being part of your family, or anyone else's. I'll never do that again. Kathy was shocked. *I haven't known him for twenty-four hours and he's talking like this?*

"I heard that! I'm never getting married either. I don't know where that came from. See what you do to me?" Deuce reacted quickly. *Damn, that was a little too quick. I'm going to have to slow it down a notch.*

"Just so you heard me.," Kathy replied, looking at the menu. "It just worried me for a minute. You hardly know me! And, I hardly know you!" Kathy continued looking at the menu and changed the subject. "Seems you know the bartender well, she must like you."

"New?" Deuce was pleased to see a jealous side of her. "That's a good story," He said as he recalled how they met. "One day after work, I came in for a beer, and she was working the bar. I called her over and asked her what her name was, 'cause I never saw her in here before. She said I'm new. Then I missed her name, so I just call her New."

His story amused Kathy *So that's how nicknames are born?* she thought. "Doesn't she mind?"

"Apparently not. She hasn't said anything."

"That's cute. She must like you." Kathy said waiting to see his reaction.

Deuce knew what she meant. To ease her mind, he added, "So does her husband. I'll have to introduce you."

Kathy was embarrassed. As she thought about it a little more, she considered New wasn't really interested in him. *You're not the best-looking guy in the joint.* Kathy's jealous side began to emerge. *Mike would have been more her style. But, with the money you throw around, you could probably attract most gold-digging sluts. Yet, there is something about you that pulls me to you, and it's certainly not the money. I've experienced money, and it never helped the relationship.* She remembered Jim, *Jim tried to buy me, own me, control me. That will never happen again.*

New returned to the table quickly with the drink. Deuce got his Bud Light with a wink, and Kathy took her Coke with a smile. New was glad to see deuce with a woman. In the few months that she had known him this was the first time he was seen courting a woman for more than just one night. He always flirted and bought drinks all around, but never with the same woman twice. *She must be a gold digger.* New thought. *Why else would she be with him? She's too pretty.*

"Do you know what you want?" New asked with her brightest smile.

"Sweetheart, what would you like?" Deuce asked Kathy as she lifted her head from the menu.

"I'll take a Black Diamond steak with a baked potato." She responded.

"What vegetable? We have corn, green beans, or broccoli/ cauliflower mix," New asked.

"Corn."

"What dressing with your salad?"

"Do me a favor, give me ranch dressing on the side, please." Kathy didn't like a lot of dressing

"Not a problem, and you sir?" New turned to Deuce.

"Everything the same, except I'll have Russian dressing." Deuce was glad Kathy didn't protest over the sweetheart comment. *Things are going as planned so far. I hopes she likes the surprise I got her.* He took her hand and smiled as he pulled a cigarette from a pack in his T-shirt pocket.

"Can I bum a cigarette from you?" Kathy asked, remembering how much better it was to kiss him having smoked as well. And, she was planning to kiss him again.

"You don't even have to ask. If you want one, just grab one from my pocket. Deuce thought of her fingers in his pocket and smiled.

"Aren't you sweet!" Kathy replied smiling, knowing she wouldn't always do that. She noticed his outfit. The same black T-shirt, with new Jeans, but no red suspenders. *He's definitely a hillbilly*, she thought. *I hope he owns more.* He also had a new dew rag which made him look like the biker dude she thought he was. And it also made him look more dangerous. But, nothing he had done so far made her feel like she was in danger. So far, he had been a true southern gentleman. Kathy lit the cigarette, remembering the menthol cigarette, she had once smoked. She knew she was going to be hooked again. But at this point she didn't care. *Perhaps that's the danger, the nicotine addiction. The moment, he's gone,* she believed, *the urge would be gone.* Until then, she decided to go with the flow.

The food arrived amid another of Deuce's stories. This story took place in Texas, where he was laying pipe in the 1980's. The story began after Kathy talked of living in Nacogdoches, Texas and how she would love to go back. Sadly, he said he was not allowed to return to Texas, because he had killed a man who brought a knife to a gunfight. He then laughed.

Feeling a twinge of anxiety again, Kathy questioned, "What was that all about?", nervous for his answer.

"Well, this "spic" thought he was king shit and was bothering a white woman at the bar. There was no reason for it, so I told him to knock it off. He clocked me. My buddies were going to ring his bell, but I told 'em it was my fight, and I would take care of it. At that time, I was smart enough to bring my pistol with me. I thought if he saw it, he would back down. So, I asked him if he wanted to take it outside. We did; he pulled out his knife so I pulled out my gun. He wasn't the ripest berry on the vine and lunged at me. It was last thing he ever did."

"I call that self-defense. So why keep you from going back to Texas?" Kathy asked. She couldn't wait to hear his reason.

"The judge said that said too. But this was Texas in the 80's. The laws are different there. Because I called him out, and not the other way around, he told to me never to come back, so I never will. Some different statute. But the judge liked me, and seemed to be a little prejudiced, and threw the case out somehow. He told me never come back." This was the story that worked well for him. *It Kathy ever knew the real reason; it would blow his plans.*

Dinner and conversation lasted for an hour. Kathy succumbed to Deuce, and had a rum and coke. When she looked at the time, she knew Shari would be waiting at the Lodge. "Deuce," she finally interjected. "Shari and John are going to the Lodge. They want to meet us there. Chances are they are already there."

"Sounds good to me. That way we don't have far to go at the end of the night. You're staying at Shari's, aren't you?" Hoping Kathy was planning to stay with him, he pulled her to his lips for a soft kiss.

"I was planning on it." She responded, a little light headed from his kiss.

Delighted with his plans being unaltered, he quickly interjected, "Whenever you're ready. Let me pay the bill and we'll go." Excusing himself from the table, he thought, *Granny Rose's special love potion will change your sleeping quarters; little do you know.*

She noticed Deuce's smile reached from ear-to-ear as he returned to the table. "What's that smile all about?" Kathy asked smiling back.

"New," he said. "She was wondering if you were my wife, just come in from West Virginia."

"What did you tell her?" Kathy didn't want to be categorized that way.

"I told him not yet, just to aggravate her." He winked at Kathy, who had lost her smile.

"You know I won't go down that road again." She wanted to make that perfectly clear.

Deuce loved the way she pulled back when he mentioned marriage. *She will never have to worry about that ever again, if all goes right,* he thought as he recalled his last prey. *But Kathy's gonna give me more of a challenge than the last one. I can see that already.*

"You know, you never told me how many times you were married." Kathy finally questioned Deuce since she already confessed hers.

"Twice, I will tell you about that later if you want to go to the Lodge before Shari and John start worrying." Deuce assumed that's why they were meeting them. Kathy was still uncomfortable with him.

Not confirming nor denying his assumption, Kathy agreed it was time to leave. Deuce walked her to her car, and opened the door. With a quick kiss, she sat in her seat and started the car. Deuce, not satisfied with the kiss she gave him, bent down, and gave her a passionate kiss. Kathy could do nothing but respond with her own fervor. Deuce quickly shut the door, leaving her wanting more.

Kathy spent the entire ride thinking about Deuce's kiss, and wondering why it had affected her the way it did. It was soft, tender, and passionate. With the twelve years of feeling asexual, she had suddenly felt emotions strange to her. The feelings of being wanted sexually sent her head spinning and impaired her judgment. She wanted Deuce to be her White Knight, but she couldn't see the black stallion he was riding.

Kathy arrived at the Lodge, just as Shari and John walked in the front door. Deuce, who seemed to drive under the speed limit the entire distance, pulled in as Kathy got to the door. She waited as he parked his car. It seemed to be an eternity before she saw him walking around the corner of the building.

"Come on old man!" she called as he appeared. She smiled as he picked up his pace.

"Old man? I'll show you old man!"

As he neared Kathy, he pulled her into his arm and smothered her with another passionate kiss. Kathy's knees became Jell-O as he held her tight to him. His kiss sent her into another world of sensations. She tingled in places left unexplored for years. She wanted more, yet guilt reared its ugly head. Just as she was ready to pull away, Deuce released her and she stumbled.

"Look at that," he said as she stumbled back into his arms. "I just saved your life." He smiled, rebalanced her, and opened the door to the Lodge. *Soon she will be mine,* he thought.

The Lodge was relatively empty compared to the Inn. Two men looking to be in their 70s, sat side-by-side at the far end of the bar, while too other young men sat separated on a couple of stools at the opposite end. Shari and John selected a table just in front of the bar, and were waving to Kathy and Deuce as they walked through the door.

"You know what you want?" Deuce asked as he pulled the chair out for Kathy.

"I think I'll try Kahlua and cream. That's not potent, is it?" She wanted to keep her wits about her tonight. Deuce seemed to have some type of power over her and she certainly didn't want to lose control.

"Nope. And can I get you two something while I'm at the bar," Deuce offered turning to Shari and John.

"Nope, we're good." John replied with a full bottle of Heineken and Shari with her full glass of rum and Coke.

Deuce walked to the bar while Kathy and Shari started to whisper and giggle. When the bartender asked what he would like, he knew, a White Russian was just what Kathy needed to loosen up. Deuce hoped she would be unaware of the added vodka, but that was easy to explain away. He ordered his usual Bud light, and quietly added a shot of tequila as a kicker. *Tonight, she'll be mine, one way or another,* he thought as the warmth of the tequila traveled its course.

Deuce sat the White Russian in front of Kathy. It was a little stronger than the Kahlua and cream she wanted, but that would be easy to explain. He pulled his seat closer to her than it was, so if there were any questions about her drink, he'd be right there to rationalize, Top Shelf Kahlua. Kathy and Shari were chatting as he sat down and was shocked to hear the word DEAD in their conversation. He listened intently to figure out what the girls had said.

"It's got to be hard." Kathy said with a sympathetic ear. "You think you'll ever go back to Texas?"

"I don't know. It's been hard since she died. I don't think I could ever go back." Shari's eyes welled up. It took over a year to be able to talk about it. Her firstborn was the first to go. She was so young when she died in a house fire.

Deuce felt a desperate need to find out the details. "Who we talk'n about? I got into this conversation too late. Is it a relative?" He asked Kathy quietly, thinking about the girl from Texas and hoping there was no coincidence.

Kathy turned to Deuce quietly told him the quick version of the story. "Shari and John's daughter died in a house fire last year. She was her firstborn."

With a sigh of relief, sounding like a sigh of pity, Deuce could only say, "Oh." He knew the chances were slim that it was the same girl, but he had to find out. He had heard her body had never been found, but that was years ago. Deuce's paranoia was getting the best of him right now, he needed to keep it in check. *This night has to go down as planned. One mistake and she gets away.*

Chapter 7

A Night at the Lodge

The night started out slow. The music on the juke box was playing Country Music, as the room filled slowly with small groups or pairs of men. Occasionally a couple would straggle in to drink only one drink, then leave. There was no dance floor to speak of, but if tables were moved, they claimed it had one.

Kathy continued to drink the Kahlua and Creams Deuce brought her. Her count had it at four. The "top shelf" Kahlua in the drinks made her head feel foggy. She listened as Deuce talked of his farm, his friends, and his escapades. Kathy was enchanted. His West Virginia dialect, made her pay close attention.

"…We had a full truck load," Deuce said after one of his adventures. He laughed. He loved getting away with something illegal. He thrived on it.

"That was the lazy man's fishing," Kathy replied with a smile.

"No, resourceful, where I come from." Deuce stood grabbing his empty cans of beer and her empty glass.

"I had enough, go-ahead, if you want one." Kathy was feeling the drinks now. In fact, after the last drink, she was feeling a little dizzy.

"This will be the last one for me," Deuce countered. "Y'all want one, don't ya?" He asked Shari and John, who seemed to be in a stupor during his stories. They were also feeling the effects of the alcohol.

Speaking for both, Shari leaned against John, "last one."

"Okay, last one." Kathy said. She only had a short distance to go to Shari's, one more wouldn't hurt.

Deuce walked away with the drink order. Kathy asked for less Kahlua this time, but he knew instead of vodka in her last drink, *Granny Rose's moonshine 150.*

John and Shari sat quietly. Shari asked first, "Kathy are you going to be okay? Shari knew Kathy had more to drink tonight then she ever saw before. She had a two-drink limit, but at that point, she noticed her feeling it.

"I'll be okay. I only have to drive less than a quarter mile to your place, and I can still feel my feet and fingers," she said jokingly. "Tell me, while he's not here, what do you think about Deuce?"

John spoke first. "Kathy, I like him. He doesn't seem to have a mean bone in his body. He's really easy going."

"He's a keeper!" Shari added.

"He's been a complete gentleman to me. He's sweet, and he's got a cute personality. Since I've gotten to know him, his age doesn't matter." Kathy loved the way Deuce complimented her, not just in words, but also in actions. Deuce was funny, kind, and generous. If she let him, he'd open every door for her.

Deuce return to the table with Shari and John's drinks first, then returned to the bar for his and Kathy's drinks. He took a few moments to spike Kathy's drink with his moonshine, hoping she wouldn't notice. If she did, he was ready with his explanation. Since she wasn't a drinker, he knew he could explain it away. Deuce showed up, smiling as he placed the drinks on the table. He sat close to Kathy, wrapping his arms around her shoulders. "I hate seeing this evening come to an end. Like I said, never met anyone like you." He whispered in Kathy's ear.

Kathy turned to him and kissed him. She allowed him to kiss her deeply, exactly what she needed. She had been tired of feeling unwanted, everything she wanted was wrapped up in this southern deep voiced gentleman. She felt as if she was under his spell. When he pulled away from the kiss, she felt a yearning for this man deep in her loins. She took a long drink from her glass as she peered into Deuce's soft blue eyes. Suddenly, she began to cough from the strength of the alcohol.

"Damn! That was a strong one!" She cried, between coughs.

"I told him it was last one for the night," Deuce explained. "He probably put extra Kahlua in your drink. Besides, you hadn't taken that big of a drink all night. Best sip it."

Of course, Kathy accepted that explanation. She hadn't taken that big of a drink before. It was amazing after she had done that, how her head started to feel it. She was convinced never do that again. Little did she know, it wouldn't matter how quickly she drank it, with each sip she got closer to forgetting the last one she took.

John and Shari finished their drinks rather quickly. They had to walk home if Kathy wasn't leaving with them. And, by the way she was hanging on Deuce, they accepted the fact, she wasn't. They knew Deuce was staying upstairs, and chances were, she was staying with him. That was probably the best since she had been drinking, and she wasn't used to it. They were worried about her safety. Deuce had treated them quite well. They hoped Kathy had finally found a man who would treat her right. As they both stood to leave, Kathy glanced up and gave them a sluggish smile.

"Where you going?" She slurred.

"We've got to get home," Shari told her. "We have to make sure the kids are okay. When you're ready to come down, the bed will be waiting."

"You want me to drive you home?" Kathy offered.

"No. We need to walk. It will give us a chance to sober up before we get home," Shari said, knowing it wouldn't be the best idea for Kathy to drive.

"Believe me, nothing is going to happen to this woman. It took me too long to find her." Deuce said that sincerely, pulling Kathy close to him. *There's no way I'm letting this one go. I'm not waiting another three years.*

Satisfied, John put his arm around Shari and bid two good night. Shari needed John's arm around her to stabilize her as she walked through the door. Kathy watched as the door shut behind them, unaware of the severity of the situation. All she knew was how Deuce was there holding her steady in her seat, while the room slowly closed in on her.

"Sweetheart, I need to go to the room before I take you home. Do you want to come see it?" Deuce asked.

Kathy heard what he had said to her, but she wasn't sure she could make it up the stairs. "Maybe I should, uh, wait, should you, uh, wait." She couldn't express herself. The alcohol caught up to her with a vengeance.

Deuce caught her in his arms as she fell sideways from her chair. "I'm not leaving you here in this condition. Someone might try to take advantage of you." He pulled her to her feet, holding her weight as he walked her up the stairs leading to his room. His room was at the far end of the hallway, so as they topped the stairs, Deuce scooped Kathy into his arms and carried her. Kathy didn't even notice and just laid her head on his shoulder, giving him full reign. Deuce loved the feeling of total control. But, all he knew was that she would be his; there was no doubt.

As soon as he reached his room, he laid Kathy on the bed and slowly disrobed her. Her top was the first to go. With each button, his penis began to swell and harden. By the time he removed her bra, he was so ready to enter her, he thought he would explode. Her breasts were firm and round, with nipples that seemed to have a natural erection. Hurriedly, he unbuttoned her shorts and slowly pulled them off, grabbing her underpants too. Kathy moaned as Deuce fell to his knees to taste the nectar between her legs. She was wet and sweet. As he lapped up the nectar, he unbuttoned his pants and allowed them to fall off. Licking her with his tongue, and stroking his penis with his hand, Deuce knew he had to introduce himself to her. With her legs open and falling off the bed, he positioned himself to enter her. Slowly he placed his throbbing penis into her wet, hot opening.

Kathy had laid silently until Deuce pushed his thick penis into her. She had been without a man for so long, she felt virgin pain all over again. But instinctively, she pulled him down on top of her searching for his mouth. Deuce complied thrusting himself into her until there was nowhere else he could go. Kissing her, thrusting, and caressing her, until he finally exploded into his own ecstasy.

Deuce continued to lay on top of Kathy, kissing her and pumping slowly. He wasn't sure it would happen, but he felt her orgasm ripple through her. She moaned with satisfaction.

"Baby, you're the one I've been looking for," he whispered in her ear. "I'm never letting you go." Deuce meant that in his own deceitful way. *Oh, how I meant that. You're gonna be mine you can't take it anymore. I can't wait to get you home. You'll be the best trophy I ever brought back to West Virginia.*

Kathy heard what Deuce said, but it seemed like a dream. She was barely conscious of what just happened. She wondered if it was a dream or had she just enjoyed a fabulous orgasm. At that point, she didn't care. It was the first orgasm she enjoyed in years, that wasn't self-imposed. At least she hoped it was. With that thought. Kathy succumbed to the darkness.

Chapter 8

Still Searching

The Communicator, **Friday March 15, 2003**

Three years have passed since a body was found on the shore of Elk river, in Clay County. Sheriff Dale Taylor responded to this reporter's inquiry, by directing me to Dr. Jake Holmes, the Clay County Coroner, who had been working on the case. Dr. Holmes replied that the case was "ongoing". No missing persons were reported in this area, and the NATIONAL MISSING PERSONS BUREAU also turned up no clues. The woman, known as Jane Doe, 11857, was buried in the Clay Cemetery, her case classified as a murder. No suspects have been identified. If any further information is received, it will be published.

Rusty read the article, remembering it to be the last case he and Jasmine responded to as a team. The investigation went cold after three months. There had been few clues left behind. The death had been ruled a homicide shortly after the body was found. Due to the numerous injuries found on the body, Doc Holmes had no choice but to declare it to be a murder.

Rusty put the paper aside and drank down the last of his coffee. Jasmine was waiting for him to take her on her daily ride. Today, he was taking her through the upper hills towards Clendenin. It was early afternoon on his day off, and he planned to spend it away from civilization. He packed his saddle bag with sandwiches and beer, as well as treats for Jasmine. He gave himself permission to avoid all responsibilities. Especially when it came to law enforcement.

Jasmine stood with her ears forward, ready for a chance to explore with her master. Rusty had saddled Jasmine earlier and left her waiting until he finished preparing for their trip. Jasmine perked her head up when she saw him carrying the saddle bag over his shoulder toward her pen.

"You ready girl?" Rusty tossed the saddle bag over Jasmine's rear and fastened it securely. Pulling himself up into the saddle, Rusty waited for Jasmine to give him her head, then he gave her the command to move forward. It only took a slight movement of his legs and buttocks for Jasmine to understand when to go forward, when to turn, and even when to stop. Jasmine would not give him her head or relax her head. Rusty dismounted as he was taught to do in this situation.

"Well, have your own way," Rusty said as he led Jasmine by the reins towards the gate of his driveway. Before they had reached it, Rusty stopped, pulling Jasmine's head downward and held it there. He stroked her neck and stood quietly. Then, he released her head, attempting again to mount her, and asking again for her head.

"You ready now?" He asked. Without hesitation, Jasmine responded and he gave his command for a forward walk. Rusty breathed a sigh of contentment at feeling Jasmine's pace, soft beneath him. He reached and stroked her neck in appreciation for allowing him to ride her. When Rusty respected her, she followed his commands.

Rusty lived in Clay County, just on the outskirts of Clendenin. The outskirts meant just before the address change from Beaumont to Clendenin. The town of Clendenin in Kanawha County extended into Clay County. His driveway began on hardtop, then extended up the mountain towards Clendenin on a gravel road, where it ended at his one-bedroom Log cabin. He had built it in 1993 after his marriage to a local girl ended. He had known her for years. She grew up in Charleston, and after a year living "out in the sticks," as she called it, she moved back to Charleston and filed for divorce. She cleaned him out both financially and emotionally. It had been ten years, now the only female in his life was Jasmine.

Before the duo got too far down the drive, Rusty chose to take the high path towards the top of the mountain. There was an open field at the top that was overgrown with shrubs and trees. The land looked barren this time of year with the brush all brown and dead. It was at this location Rusty gave Jasmine a treat, allowing her to run. Jasmine knew the way, so Rusty sat back in the saddle and allowed her to lead the way.

As Jasmine reached the edge of the field, Rusty noticed her pace increase without waiting for his command. She had never begun her run unless Rusty gave her the command. Once he was ready, she began to gallop. This was the moment Rusty loved the most. This was the time he felt as one with Jasmine. The field was a good acre, and they took two laps around its perimeter. Rusty asked Jasmine to slow to a trot with a simple movement and she responded. As she slowed to a comfortable speed, Rusty saw a path he had never noticed before. It seemed to run parallel with the top of the mountain. For a change of scenery, he guided Jasmine towards it. As they approached the beginning of the trail, Rusty motioned Jasmine to stop. Before they ventured on the new trail, Rusty thought it was best to walk Jasmine, rather than ride her. The last thing he wanted to do, was to injure her because of hidden obstacles.

Rusty dismounted Jasmine. Before he moved on, he pulled the saddle bag off her rump and opened it. There were two beers and two sandwiches, plus an apple for Jasmine. He pulled out one beer, one sandwich, and the apple for Jasmine. He tapped the top of his beer, sat it on the ground. beside him, and stroked Jasmine's neck.

"Girl, you deserve this," he said as he held the apple to Jasmine's mouth. By the time she had finished chomping the apple down, Rusty knew he could open his beer without losing any through a carbonated blast. He unwrapped his sandwich and reached for his beer. As he touched the can he noticed a sparkle of silver beneath it. *An old coin*, he thought as he picked up the can. With his boot, he scuffed the dirt to loosen it from its cocoon. As he kicked the dirt away, the silver became thicker than a coin. The design became more delicate than that of a coin. He stopped kicking it for fear of damaging it anymore. He stopped and pried it out with his fingers, and a chain followed. *It's a locket. What's a locket doing out here? I bet some teenagers were here for their first encounter.* He smiled as it brought back his own memory of losing his virginity and taking hers.

Rusty picked up his beer and popped the tab, holding on to the locket's chain, allowing it to dangle as he took a large swallow. When it hit his chin in one of its swings, he opened his eyes instinctively. *What is that?* He saw markings that looked like a name and a date, but the dirt obscured the lettering. He dropped it into the palm of his hand and began to pour the beer on top of it. Now, the dirt was mud and he began to swirl it with his thumb. With a swipe on his pants, a name appeared.

Margret J. Morrill, the inscription read. The date, **02-14-60** was also seen beneath the name. It was the date received or the birth date, Rusty wasn't sure. With the dirt loosened, Rusty decided to open the locket to see if there was a picture inside. With his left hand, he carefully leveraged his thumb nail between the top and bottom. A pop and it was opened. Suddenly, a faded picture of a beautiful blonde with a wide smile was looking up at him. *How long have you been here?* She looked familiar to him. *She must be a local.*

Rusty stopped to enjoy his second beer and sandwich before walking Jasmine onto the new path. He was surprised to find the trail end on the road just above his driveway. *Must be a deer run*, he concluded as he mounted Jasmine for the last hundred yards of their ride. "Let's leave that trail for the deer Jasmine. We've got others. Sure was worth the walk though." He said as he patted his pocket with his new find.

Chapter 9

Convinced

Morning came with the warmth of sunshine. Bright light was pouring through the blinds. Her head ached, her ears hurt, and her eyes felt swollen. Beside her lay Deuce, buck naked. She looked beneath the covers and found herself in the same state. She moved as little as possible, as not to awaken the man next to her. The night was not a dream. The orgasm was not imagined. She realized the alcohol had overcome her inhibitions and the guilt began to seep into her soul.

"Good morning beautiful," Deuce said softly, knowing she probably had a hangover. "How ya feel'n'?"

Kathy was startled to hear his voice. He had been waiting for her slightest movement. "So-so. My head is killing me." She replied in a barely audible voice.

"I've got something for that." Deuce turned to the side of the bed, and pulled a small brown bottle from his jeans, which laid on the floor. "Just take a sip," he told her as he handed her the bottle of moonshine. "This is a recipe my Granny Rose used for hangovers when grandpa had them."

Kathy reluctantly took the bottle, opened it, and took a whiff of its contents. "This smells awful!" She complained, feeling a wave of nausea. "What's in it?"

"Just say it's old-fashioned moonshine. If you want I'll take a sip first to show you it's not poison," Deuce offered. "Believe me, within ten minutes, the hangover will be gone. They call it the Hair of the

Dog." He smiled at Kathy and extended his hand for the bottle. "Let me show ya."

"No, I believe you." Hopefully it would remove the tremendous pain. Kathy tipped the bottle to her lips, and allowed a sip to pollute her palate. The taste was horrid, and her face winced as she swallowed. Kathy felt the need to be sick and hoped the look of disgust wouldn't be obvious. She mentally reprimanded herself, as she softly laid back on the pillow.

"Here, wash it down with this," Deuce said as he offered her a drink from a warm can of Bud Light. He knew the taste was one of the worst you could contend with, especially after a night of drinking; but he also knew it would do the trick.

Appreciative, Kathy sat up and took the drink he offered. Although the beer was warm, it masked the taste enough to be tolerated. Then, placing her head on his warm chest, she wrapped her arms around him. He placed the can on the side table as Kathy closed her eyes, waiting for the throbbing to stop.

"Baby," Deuce said in his soft southern drawl. "You are the most amazing woman I've ever met." He softly kissed the top of her head. "When you're ready, we can go get something to eat downstairs. Right now, I want you to rest while I jump in the shower. You can get yours when you're ready."

"Can you grab my bag out of the car for me before you get in the shower?" Kathy asked as Deuce rolled out of bed.

"You got it girl. Give me a minute and I'll go down before I jump in the shower." Deuce walked into the bathroom as Kathy watch him strut his naked body through the bathroom door, failing to close it behind him.

With the sound of never ending relief echoing through the room, Kathy felt her own need to urinate bubbling below. She listened intently for Deuce to finish so she could do the same. Scooting to the bottom of the bed, Kathy feared losing it as had happened in the past. Spastic Bladder Syndrome, *didn't take my pill. My luck, I'll piss myself and puke at the same time!*

Passing Deuce in the doorway, Kathy exclaimed, "The car keys are in my shorts." Hurriedly, she made her way to the toilet, losing it as she sat. If she had waited much longer, there would have been a stream leading to the seat.

Kathy had yet to tell Deuce about her M.S. and wished she would have done it before they had sex. She looked around for signs of a condom, but saw none. *Well, why not.* She shook her head. *With my luck, I just contracted my death sentence. Fuck, Fuck. Why not. No-one more deserving!* Tears filled her eyes. *God, I hate myself.* She returned to the bed, and crawled beneath the sheets to cry.

Deuce returned a short time later to find Kathy beneath his sheets. He smiled seeing her so vulnerable. *This is where I want you, in my bed,* He thought. *And this is where you'll be for as long as you can take it.*

Kathy, oblivious to his return, snoozed to the shower's hum. By the time Deuce emerged from the shower, Kathy had recovered from her hangover just as Deuce had predicted. She pulled herself to the end of the bed and pulled her clothes from her bag. She felt dirtier than expected. Then she wondered if this was just a one night stand? Guilt, despair, and fear ate at her soul.

"Need my help?" Deuce asked playfully. "I'd be glad to wash your back, or anything else you'd like." He gave her a bright smile with a twinkle in his eyes.

"I think I can manage. My headache is gone, just like you said. What was that I drank?" Kathy, smiled as she remembered how much she liked Deuce. She disguised her thoughts for that instance, recalling how wonderful he made her feel.

"Granny Rose's Moonshine," he said with a smile. "Told you it would work." He was so proud of Granny Rose. She lived through so much surviving many years serving her shine, especially after his grandfather was killed. Deuce never forgot catching up to those murderers. Seeing them beg for their lives as he dismembered them limb by limb. It was a memory he cherished *It was a shame,* he thought. *They couldn't see their own head come off.*

Deuce, and his brothers, were raised by his grandmother after they had lost their parents in an arson fire. This, combined with his grandfather's murder, was the root to all his killing. To date, he had killed, five men and two women. The women in memory of Granny Rose, who was the pinnacle of all women. The two men that set the fire, and the ones who killed his grandfather. Killing had become second nature, disposing of the bodies was ingenious, no one had ever found the remains of any of his victims, as far as he knew. Because West Virginia was a vast wilderness, he believed they never would. *And if they did, they would have their work cut out for them*, he thought.

While Kathy showered, Deuce fought the urge to follow her. Quietly he opened the door to peek at her shadow behind the shower curtain. She was in the process of washing her hair. She was facing towards him as she scrubbed her head. As she turned to rinse, he strolled quietly to the curtain, peering in at her glistening body. He watched the stream of water as it rolled down her well-defined spine to the drain. Her red hair was longer wet, as the weight of the water pulled the curls into longer strands. He wanted to grab her and take her on the bathroom floor. But, the next time he wanted her to give herself willingly. That was the next step in his plan, which seemed be to running its course flawlessly.

As Kathy finished rinsing her hair, Deuce closed the curtain and walked out, closing the door behind him. Kathy felt a chill as the door closed and she turned to look. There was no one there but her. She shook her head in disbelief. *Was I just being paranoid?* she thought as she stepped out of the shower. She dried off and dressed in the bathroom out of modesty, even though she knew he had already seen all of her. All the years of feeling unattractive had embedded itself in her. She tried to shake that feeling, but feared she would never be able to shake it.

Deuce waited patiently for Kathy to emerge from the shower. He sat on the edge of the bed planning his next seduction. He knew Kathy would leave sometime today and he wanted desperately to have her one more time before she left. *Stand down Sergeant.* He told himself. *You have plenty of time.* Deuce knew, if he rushed, Kathy would pull away. There was something in her that made him think she was a runner, and not the apathetic type.

Kathy joined Deuce on the bed. Dressed in tan shorts and a sleeveless white shirt, her towel dried wet hair, fell into wet curls. Deuce couldn't help noticing her innocence. She never dressed seductively or sleazy, but radiated a gentle sweetness inside a pleasing package.

"You're the prettiest thing I've seen in all my travels. Hell, the women in Paris don't hold a candle to you." Deuce bushed her hair back and kissed her neck. Her fresh clean scent began to arouse him.

Kathy, feeling the softness of his lips with the tickle of his mustache, closed her eyes in sweet surrender. He slipped his hand behind her back as she turned to engulf his passionate kiss. she felt her nipples begin to rise as his hand began to caress them. She knew they had already had sex, but still had apprehensions like it was the first time, because she couldn't remember the night before.

Deuce realized how Kathy responded to his kiss. He grabbed her hand and led it to the bulge in his pants. "You are the first person to arouse me like you do." He whispered softly in her ear. "After the stroke, I never thought I could get Henry working again."

Kathy took his growing appendage and stroked it slowly. She knew she wanted him again. It had been so many years without a man's loving touch. She wanted to remember it this time. She unbuttoned and unzipped his pants, continuing to kiss him passionately. Their kiss was in sync and it sent her into a fantastic world of sweet sensations.

Deuce wasted no time and pulled his pants off his hips. Slipping his hands under Kathy's shirt, he slowly pulled it over her head, pausing to kiss her. Skillfully he unfastened her bra and without missing a beat, she allowed it to fall to the floor. Deuce stopped abruptly and pushed Kathy down onto the bed, climbing beside her, rather than on top of her. As Kathy continued to fondle him, increasing his arousal, Deuce continued kissing her passionately, plunging his tongue ever deeper. He made no effort to remove her shorts, then he broke away for just enough time to remove his shirt so he could feel her breasts against his chest. With an all-in attitude, Kathy finally unbuttoned her pants. Deuce was more than ready and he forced his hand down her pants as she pulled them off. Kathy was wet with excitement and Deuce slid his finger into her, pulling it out for a taste.

"You taste so good," he said in a soft voice. He pulled himself up as if to mount her, but took the lower road first. He was eager to taste more of her. Putting his head between her legs, he began to tantalize her with his tongue.

Kathy felt Deuce's enjoyment, and it peaked her excitement. She didn't want to come however; not that way. After allowing him to enjoy her for a short time, Kathy pulled him up. Deuce agreed and inserted his swollen member into her wet, tight opening. The fit was snug, and Kathy felt every motion. Deuce wasn't in a hurry, like she had experienced with Carl, but with rhythmic motion so to please her. With each pound to her clitoris, Kathy knew she would climax. She did, allowing Deuce to feel the ripples and his explosion followed. Together they enjoyed the wonders of their own sexuality.

Shortly after their pleasure, Deuce and Kathy walked together, hand in hand, down the stairs to Sunday breakfast. They each ordered the infamous "Big Breakfast." This contained: two eggs. Hash browns, three strips of bacon, coffee, and toast. Kathy nervously looked at her watch, remembering she hadn't called Jeff.

"Late for an appointment?" Deuce asked seeing her look at the watch.

"No, I just forgot to call home to tell Jeff I was staying the night because I drank too much to drive. He probably called Shari. I'll have to call him." Kathy was worried how he would react. Since his father walked out, he had been volatile.

"How old is he?" Deuce asked.

"Eighteen going on ten," she commented. Kathy felt trapped by her own guilt when it came to Jeff. His Psychologist suggested using Natural Consequences to help Jeff control his impulsiveness. Kathy wanted to see him succeed so badly. Feeling alone in the battle, she knew she gave him too much control. But, he was eighteen. *Buttons; he knows my buttons*!

"I know the type. They'd bitch if they were hung with a new rope." Deuce didn't want any competition.

"You'd think." Kathy said nothing more on the subject, she never knew what to say about her son's behavior. Diagnosed with A.D.H.D. at an early age, Jeff attended countless appointments with Psychologists, Social Workers, and Religious counselors. Still, she never knew what to expect. Medications caused side effects that he could not tolerate. A fear, no matter how unreasonable, paralyzed him. Soon, he'd be leaving. But oh, how she feared it. Awful scenarios bounced around in her head when he talked about it. *I wish men knew what type of damage they did to their children, especially their son, when they abandoned them. A never-ending pain and anger seethes inside them. Self-blame becomes an overwhelming fear in trusting themselves and others. Society often receives the short end of the stick.* Anger and despair replaced the pleasure she felt moments before.

Breakfast passed without incident. As Deuce paid the bill, Kathy decided the best thing she could do was go home. She decided not to go to Shari's, knowing she'd have to answer endless questions about the night before. She still wasn't sure how she felt about it. All she knew was, *she wanted to see Deuce again.* He made her feel wanted for the first time in a long time. His deep southern drawl was just the icing on the cake.

Kathy stood as Deuce returned to the table. "Where do you want to go?" Deuce asked seeing her standing and ready to go.

"I'm ready to go home. Maybe I can get home before Jeff wakes up and I can avoid any explanation. I'll just tell him I got in late."

"Why do you think you have to explain anything? He knew you were coming to the Lake." Deuce saw she was wrapped around Jeff's finger. *This kid has her wrapped around his little finger. I'm gonna have to meet this one."*

"I know I don't have to, but I'd rather avoid his temper." Kathy remembered holes in the walls after many of his temper tantrums and she feared she would be his next wall.

"He's working, isn't he?" Deuce asked. Why doesn't he get an apartment?"

He works for Ames part-time. Minimum slave-labor pay. He couldn't buy a pot to piss in." She explained.

"Well, he could find a better job. Can he weld?" Deuce figured he may as well ask.

"Trade school would be great, but he's fighting it." Kathy felt helpless. With Carl out of the picture, no financial support, and no emotional support, she was left to deal with her son alone. Her job at the Insurance Company paid just enough to cover her bills. Without Carl's contribution, she was planning to move. The trick was to move Jeff out first.

With her son in the picture, Kathy would be thrilled with the trip she'll be taking. A change of scenery will be an easy sell. Deuce loved seeing his plan come together. *You watch'n' over me Granny?*

Walking and talking, hand in hand, they reached Kathy's car. "How far do you have to go to get home?" Deuce asked.

"Oh, about 30 miles. I never really measured it. Why?" Kathy asked.

"Would you mind if I came over? I'd really like to meet this boy of yours."

"When? Next week?" Kathy wanted Deuce to meet her son one day if the relationship continued.

"I'd love to spend the day with you, and if you don't mind, I'd like to see how to find the place. I'm still not familiar with the area." Deuce hoped Kathy would agree. Helplessness seemed to work before.

Kathy took a moment to ponder the idea. Spending the day with him was something she would like. If Jeff liked Deuce, he might not be so pissed off. And, he wouldn't blow up at her when she got home. "Sounds good to me. Let me get my bag and we can get going."

Deuce escorted Kathy to his room, via the back steps, and then back down to the steps to her car. *This is going well. In fact, ahead of schedule. I don't know how I got this lucky. It took weeks for the last one.* Deuce was pleased with himself. *The alignment never left him down.*

Deuce made sure he opened the door for Kathy. "You'll have to take it slow. I'd hate to lose you. If you noticed, I like to keep it at, or below the speed limit."

"Don't worry you won't lose me," she replied with a smile. "I'll even go under the speed limit to make sure." Kathy was certain she wanted to see where this relationship was going. Her only apprehension was the thought of Deuce being around only for sex. Still at this point, it was all good. She was still insecure and suffering from low self-esteem that had been etched into her being for so long, the lines in her face started to match the fissures in her heart.

Chapter 10

Home visit

The drive was tedious. With each mile, the twinge in her chest increased. The closer she got to Bloomsburg, the tighter her stomach felt. By the time she had reached Interstate 80, she realized how close she was to home. Images flashed through her mind. *I'm finally experiencing a touch of happiness, and Carl is going to fuck it up.* It never fails. Defeatism, despair, despondency, desolation; Kathy was the queen of those feelings. *I'm just happy to be happy. That's all God, she prayed. I'm a good person. I believe. I'm spiritual. Where are you? They say you're only given what you can handle, can you make the next thing good? I really can't handle anymore.*

Kathy and Deuce pulled slowly into the Mobile Home park. It had been a thirty-minute drive. Kathy worried about how Deuce would react to her home, considering he owned a farm on 300 acres. She imagined he would hate dating a woman who lived in a 'trailer park.' The thought of the trailer trash stereotype, began to seep into the picture. Her home, larger than most, had a front deck, accented with flowers and a blueberry bush, situated on a corner lot. *I never wanted to live in a trailer. I swore up and down, I never would. Fucking Carl wore me down. Get a trailer, land, then build. Where was he when it came to making the mortgage payments? I'm never going to be able to keep it*!

Kathy pulled into her driveway, with Deuce pulling in beside her. Before she opened her door, the front door opened and Jeff pounded out onto the porch, ready to rip her apart. She sat there long enough however, for Deuce to walk around the back of her car. With one look at him, Jeff quickly changed his expression from rage to *I'm glad you're home safe mom*. Kathy got when Deuce opened her door offering her his hand.

"Mom, I wondered what happened to you." Jeff took on the worried about you look. He knew it wouldn't be smart to spout-off to Kathy with someone present. "I waited up for you."

"No need to be worrying, she was safe." Deuce put his arm around Kathy possessively. "Ain't noth'n going to happen to her if I have anything to do 'bout it!" Deuce walked her to the porch and extended his hand to Jeff. "Name's Deuce." Jeff shook it.

"Jeff." Deuce's Drawl took Jeff by surprise. "Where you from?" he inquired.

"West by God Virginia." Deuce stated proudly.

"He's working on a pipeline going through the state," Kathy interjected.

"Cool!" Jeff glanced at Kathy with a subtle disapproving wince. She knew the look, it was easy for her to spot.

"Met your mom at Larry's Inn there in Larrysville. She took my breath away and I'm still looking for it." Deuce smiled at Kathy with a big smile. "Been all over the world and never met nobody like her." He grabbed her hand and softly squeezed it. "Mind if I come in for a spell?" Deuce asked. He wanted to show respect by asking Jeff's permission.

"I don't care." Jeff was curious about this Southerner. *What the hell does she see in this one?* Jeff stepped aside allowing Kathy and Deuce to enter.

Deuce walked through the front door, following Kathy, who guided him to the kitchen. Kathy said, "pick your seat." Then she realized how it sounded when she saw Deuce's crooked smile as he literally picked his seat. "Smart ass! You know what I mean." Kathy matched his crooked smile as she felt a release of tension.

The table was wooden with three chairs and a bench seat. Deuce elected to sit on the bench side of the table, facing the living room and the front door. This was a natural habit, always being aware of possible oncoming enemies, and he was sure Jeff was one of them. Deuce glanced around at the state of affairs. The Mobile home was bigger than most and quite nice. There were two dogs; one was pure black, and the other a tri color. They were well behaved for their size, and gave Deuce more attention than required.

"What's their names?" Deuce asked Kathy and she placed her bag in front of the door he assumed was her bedroom.

"Bea is the black one. She is part Boxer and black lab. Rufus is part German and Australian Shepherd." Kathy loved those dogs. She had spent a lot of time training them. "We got Bea in Texas while we were there. I told you about Nacogdoches." Then she added, "you ought to hear her bark!"

"Why?" Deuce asked thinking a bark is a bark.

"She has a southern drawl just like you." She just had to say that. Comedy always seemed to break the ice. They both laughed.

"Your good. I think you missed your callin'." Deuce was really starting to realize how lucky he was to find her. *Those planets really are mysterious, and this time they're lucky.* In his mind, the only thing controlling his life at this moment, was the alignment. Deuce thought about how the dogs fit the into the picture. He knew they couldn't come with her when she came to West Virginia and she seemed quite attached to them. *Ah, just another challenge.*

"Mom, dad called," Jeff reported as he sat on the couch listening to the conversation and interjecting just to cause problems. "He called last night and left a message on the machine. He said he wanted you to call him. He left a number. I tried to call it last night when I got home, but there was no answer."

"I thought he wasn't around anymore," Deuce said remembering how Kathy said she hadn't heard from him since he left. He didn't want any more problems than he already had.

"Figures. I don't even know if I want to talk to him," she responded to Jeff. Kathy knew she would have to, but the timing was on uncanny. My luck continues, she thought. Suddenly the He-Haw song; *If it weren't for bad luck, I'd have no luck at all. Blues, despair, and agony on me*, echoed through her mind.

"Just call him mom. Or I will!" Jeff challenged Kathy, giving her no choice.

"Later. I'd hate to spoil my day so soon." Kathy was embarrassed by the way Jeff was treating her.

"If you want me to leave, I will. I don't want to stand in your way." Deuce hoped that the offer would be refused. But, even if it wasn't, he wasn't going to let this one go.

"No, I'm not going there. I'll call him later. I don't want to you to leave. I'll call him later. And Jeff, just let it go for now. I'm not going to drop everything to call him back now."

"God, damn it mom, just call." Jeff was showing disrespect for Kathy.

"Boy, that's no way to talk to your mom. If I had ever talked to my mom like that, she'd have whipped my ass. Even at your age." Deuce looked at Kathy, who looked at Jeff for a reaction.

Jeff was shocked even though Kathy had told him about how he was treating her.

It took Deuce every sense of control to keep his composure. Under normal circumstances, he would have belted Jeff a good one. *Stand down, stand down*, he repeated to himself.

"*Fuck you*," he said under his breath as he walked out of the living room and into his bedroom.

"I'm really sorry about that," Kathy said feeling humiliated. Jeff's reaction was nothing new. Since his return from lockup, his anger continued to grow. She was so tired of it, but she was helpless. She continued to rationalize it as a temporary reaction to Carl leaving. "I have never been so… embarrassed."

"You don't have to apologize for him. By what you told me, it sounds like he needs an attitude adjustment. Somethin' his dad should have done long ago." Deuce understood her embarrassment, but he also knew it could play to his advantage.

"Carl never could be a real father to Jeff. He was always too busy running with his friends. He would take Jeff with him occasionally, but he was never consistent, usually when he had no other choice." Kathy painfully remembered his lack of parenting skills. Even with all the counseling, Carl would never take advice or constructive criticism when it came to dealing with Jeff's special problem. It had made the marriage more distant. Avoidance was his way of dealing with problems, so much so, that he pulled away.

"He sounds like a real piece of work." Deuce heard what Kathy was saying, but he really didn't care. Carl wouldn't interfere with his plans, that was apparent, nor would her son. Kathy was at a place in her life that he could handle. The lonely, needy women that fate always placed at his fingertips at the exact moment the planets lined up.

Kathy knew exactly what he was talking about and had no response. She quickly changed the subject, "So what do you think about this place? Not bad for a mobile home, is it?"

"I like it. It's bigger than most. What size is it?"

"Sixteen by 80 feet. It has three bedrooms and two baths. Jeff has a bedroom at the far end while I have bedroom at this end. It also has a utility room behind you, just before the bedroom. You want to check it out?" Kathy, who had been standing at the kitchen sink, wanted him to see how big it really was.

"Sure." Deuce stood as Kathy walked behind him. He grabbed her and quickly pulled her lips to his. He wanted her to know that nothing had changed when it came to his attraction to her.

Kathy pointed out the utility room as she passed by the opening which was covered by a curtain she had hung. Opening the door to the bedroom, the unmade bed was the first thing seen. It was elevated an extra foot and a half to accommodate Carl's height. She hoped it would help the marriage as they slept on a bed like this on a trip to the Jersey Shore. *Wrong again,* she thought.

"I like the bed," Deuce commented. "Is that a water bed frame?"

"No, a wooden frame Carl built." Kathy didn't add any explanation except, "It's kind of nice not being on the floor with a standard frame."

"We definitely have to try that out." Deuce thought of the wonderful positions they could try with the elevation. Kathy didn't respond to this comment but continued the tour by showing him the bathroom with the garden tub. "Now that's what I'm talkin' about. Two can fit in there! You want to try?" Deuce pulled her into his arms giving her a kiss that expressed his playful nature. He knew she would decline his offer, but he had to try.

Kathy loved that thought. Carl would never shower with her. To her it was the most sensual feeling having the man she loved share the warmth of the water and the slick soft feeling of soaping each other up. The special foreplay, which led to fabulous sex. *It's so nice Deuce still had that youthful attitude.*

"You know, any other time I would jump at it. Too bad I already took a shower today," Kathy teased. "But maybe next time we can." Kathy kissed him with a long soft kiss.

"It wouldn't be to get clean sweetheart." Kathy smiled at his response as he scooped her up and carried her to his personal garden. Deuce felt in total control. *She is so mine. Granny you'd be so proud! Quick and easy. Smart not long.* He placed her gently on her bed. Not too high, not too low, just right. Just as he began to slide beside her, still kissing her; a knock shattered the moment.

"Oh shit. Now what?" Kathy was shocked Jeff decided to interrupt. "It's always one thing or another." Kathy pulled herself away and walked to the door. Opening it just enough to see Jeff getting ready to knock again, "what do you need?"

"Can I use the car tonight? I want to go see Jennifer after work? I be home by midnight. That's her curfew."

"What time do you get done working?" Kathy inquired.

"My shift starts at five and ends at nine. Jennifer is meeting me after work."

Kathy took the moment to think. If she timed it right, she could have dinner prepared and served before he had to leave. She knew the duty of a mom came before a new relationship. It's not that hard to decide. "Just let me grab some food for dinner, and the car is all yours. Got any ideas for dinner?"

Jeff smiled and replied, "Corn on the cob, chicken, and that dream whip salad you make. Could you pick up a watermelon too?" Jeff acted giddy knowing he not only got the car, but also his favorite meal. The dream whip salad was one of his favorites; the car, he knew she would give up. His night was set.

Kathy was relieved. Anger avoided. "Cool deal. It'll only take me a minute and I'll go get dinner. Okay?"

"Deal!" Jeff pivoted quickly and pranced away in his own victory walk.

"Sorry Deuce, let's plan this for later. I need to go out and get something for dinner. Jeff is going to use the car tonight, so I have to go get something before he leaves."

"Not a problem. We've got lots of time. We'll have lots of time to ourselves later. You know anywhere I can get a six-pack?" Normally deuce opted for a 12-pack, but since he was planning a stop at Larry's Inn after he left for home, he settled for half. Besides, he hated the thought of getting pulled over for DUI, especially since he had already lost his driver's license. That was the reason he drove so cautiously. He hated the idea of spending another night in the local jail.

"I'm not really sure. We just moved here at the end of May. I don't usually drink, but give me a minute and I'll find somewhere in the phone book." Kathy shot another quick kiss and led him by the hand into the kitchen. She looked in the phone book, Deuce sat at the kitchen table lighting a cigarette, glancing around for any sign of an ash tray. Kathy saw his dilemma and pulled out a saucer from under her dying, neglected violet, and placed it in front of him.

"That'll work," he replied.

Under 'Bars' in the Yellow Pages, Kathy found the closest one. With a few directions and a kiss, Deuce left, walking to the door, hand in hand with Kathy. "Don't you be getting me lost girl. You glad to see me leave?"

"Oh, come on. You afraid to get lost?" She replied.

Deuce loved her spirit. Fighting the urge to scoop her up, he gave her a quick kiss and headed to his car.

Kathy was glad he did not try to convince her into going with him. She felt there were some quick cleanup she could do while he was gone. She hadn't counted on company before she left on Saturday, and the dishes were piled high in the sink. Quickly she rinsed the dishes off, and placed them in the dishwasher. She then turned to the living room and picked up all the clothing Jeff left lying around the room. He evidently slept on the couch the night before. Kathy picked up and folded the blanket left behind.

"Who the hell did you bring home!" Jeff bellowed, startling Kathy. "What are you now, a slut?"

Kathy was not used to the abusive language. Her blood began to boil. Trying to keep her composure, Kathy calmly responded with his name "Deuce." She refused comment on the slut comment.

"What? Did you spend the night with him last night?"

"Listen Jeff, it's none of your business what I do. What, do you think I should pine away for Carl?"

"Jesus Christ mom, it's only been one month. He'll never want you back now," Jeff responded disgustedly.

"Do you think I would ever want him back? He treated me like shit. He treated you like shit too! Did you forget that?" Jeff's face told Kathy he heard what she said. "You have to forget about him coming back, Jeff, and get used to seeing me with other men. I'm not going to become some cat lady whose only companion needs a litter box."

After a moment of consideration, Jeff responded, "You could be a dog lady instead of a cat lady, mom." A smile broke out on his face. Understanding the gleam in his eyes, Kathy knew he understood.

"Listen, you have to sit down and talk to Deuce. He has the greatest stories I've ever heard." Kathy hoped Jeff would give Deuce a chance, although she knew he would only be around for a month. She was glad for his company no matter. "Oh, watch what you say around him. He didn't like what you said to me or how you said it. Give me a break. If you can't say something nice, don't say anything."

"Sorry mom. I was worried. I hate being here alone sometimes." Jeff's tone changed dramatically. A calmness enveloped him as his face soften. "I like his accent. Where's he from?"

"West Virginia. Well, by what he says, "West by God Virginia."

"Anywhere near Washington D.C.?"

"No, West Virginia, not western Virginia." Kathy had experienced that confusion while doing research during her college years. A state employee she called for information confused the two as well. "Now you see why I was concerned when you didn't come home that one night. At least you knew I was at the lake!"

The sound of Deuce's car pulling into the driveway motivated Kathy to shove the folded blanket into Jeff's arms. "Put it in your room for me." Surprisingly Jeff did exactly as she asked.

She turned and went to the door to meet Deuce. By the time she opened the door, Deuce had reached the steps to the porch. Kathy saw him carrying a tall slender bag with what appeared to be a bottle of wine, and a short grocery bag which appeared to be half full. "Change your mind about the beer?"

Deuce smiled at the thought. *Right, forgot the beer.* "Nope."

"What's the bottle?" Kathy was aware beer came in bottles, and knew the green hue of the bottle and the shape did not point to beer.

"It's wine for you. The other bag has the beer." Deuce smiled at how naïve she appeared. *She said she hadn't drank much. I guess that's a good thing.*

"You didn't have to do that." The thought humbled Kathy. It was the first time a man had bought her wine since an ex-love showed up with red wine and a yellow rose. It was the right time, but she let him get away. She was aware of that. He was the most romantic man she had ever known. It really stung after she heard he had become rich.

"You're right, I didn't have to, but I wanted to." Deuce was aware of the seductive materials needed to entice women. Today wine, tomorrow flowers. Women, in his eyes, were so predictable. First jewelry and perfume, then money. It never failed him yet and he doubted it would.

Kathy held the door open for Deuce. He refused to enter, propping the door open with his elbow, waiting for her to walk in first. Kathy may have thought this was just one of his gentlemanly ways, but Deuce and took safety factors into account. Two unfamiliar dogs in and out of control and Jeff were his motivations.

"We are going to chill the wine," Kathy said as he handed her the bag with the wine. "Since it's almost 1 o'clock, do you want me to throw something together for lunch?"

"I don't think so. Ya' know any where we can go eat close by?" Deuce asked while he pulled the six pack from his bag.

"I should still make something for Jeff." Kathy's slipped the bottle, bag, and all, onto the top shelf of the refrigerator, taking stock of how little food there was.

"Bring 'em along. No need in letting him behind." Deuce hoped to have a chance to win him over. *With that feat accomplished, I'll be able to put my plan into action,* he thought as he popped open a can of beer. *I'm gonna get myself moved in here by the end of the month.*

As if he had radar, Jeff walked into the living room, which opened to the kitchen. "Yeah mom, you shouldn't leave me behind." It's is a blessing and a curse to live in such small quarters; very few conversations could be private.

"Jeff, where is a good place to eat 'round here?" Deuce asked.

"There is a Bonanza up by the mall." Jeff knew where he wanted to eat as soon as he heard "Go eat."

"Sounds good. Do you know if they have fried chicken livers?" This was one of his favorites.

"I don't know; I haven't been there for a long time." Jeff replied.

"I guess we gotta go check, don't we?" Deuce turned to Kathy, "What you say mom?"

"Looks like a go to me. Whenever you're ready." Kathy wasn't sure how she felt about Jeff going along, but at this point there was no hope of backing out. She thought it might be for the best. If Jeff and Deuce hit it off. Jeff may not have a problem with her dating him while he was around. But on the other hand, if they didn't click, there would be hell to pay.

"We can go as soon as I finish my beer and one more cigarette. If it's okay with you. You may want to put something on for the ladies, Jeff. From what I've seen in my travels there is always at least one nice looking waitress." Deuce appealed to his testosterone. *He's 18 and full of come. This'll be a breeze.*

Without a word, Jeff popped to his feet nearly sprinting to his room. This had been the best offer all day. He decided to dress for work, but added extra flair for tonight. Luckily, he had already showered, thinking he would have to leave early for work.

While Jeff dressed, Kathy sat beside Deuce at the table. "Can I bum a cigarette from you?" She asked.

"Anything I have is yours. If you ever need one feel free to just get into my pocket and grab one," Deuce said with a glimmer in his eyes. He skillfully pulled a cigarette from his pack and lit it for her. *Eventually she'll feel comfortable enough to help herself,* he hoped and looked forward to it.

"You're a bad influence, do you know that?"

"Thank you very much, I resemble that comment." Deuce laughed. *If she only knew.*

The two smoked their cigarettes as Deuce drank his beer, both lost in their own thoughts. One thinking a possible relationship, the other looking to complete a plan.

The music that had been playing in Jeff's room was shut off. Jeff walked out in black pants with a black silk shirt, displaying a red dragon. He was ready to go. "Ready?"

"Two more gulps and I'll be," Deuce said as he continued to drink his beer to the last drop. "You're looking pretty good there Jeff."

"I like that shirt Jeff. Did you get it at Ames?" She knew they were having a close-out sale and hoped he took advantage with his employee discount.

"Yep. It was normally $25. I got it for $15," He responded proudly.

"I' have to get there one of these days," Kathy said to herself aloud.

"Here's your chance. I have to be to work by four."

"Well I'm ready," Deuce swallowed. "Kathy, do you want to drive?"

"Yep." Kathy, who had left her keys in the car as usual, did a quick visual search. "You ready Jeff?" Everyone agreed and they made their way to the car.

Chapter 11
Dinner and Stories

Thankful the restaurant wasn't crowded, the three were seated immediately. As they passed the buffet, Deuce spotted the chicken livers he had asked about. He had grown up on chicken livers and pinto beans. Brown beans as they were referred to, were the mainstay in many homes in West Virginia. Brown beans were cooked all day in water with ham hocks. Once reduced to a thick soup, fresh onions were chopped up and used to garnish the soup. Cornbread, also a staple, helped sop up any juices left behind. Deuce doubted he would find it this far north, but he always could show Kathy how to make it for him. *She'll have to know anyways*, he thought after he eyed the soups at the buffet. *I'll wait for the next visit. She can make me some Brown beans and chicken livers for her first meal for me.* Deuce saw his plan unfolding in front of his eyes. He smiled.

All three sat in a small booth towards the back of the restaurant, Kathy and Deuce sat side-by-side, with Jeff directly across from his mother. Conversation began with a story from Deuce which was directed towards Jeff.

"Ya' know, I started working for the pipeline 'bout your age. Me and my brothers all worked on the pipeline. Do you know 'bout the Alaskan pipeline?" Deuce paused for his response which consisted of a simple nod of his head. "I worked on that back in the 70's when it first got started." Deuce wanted Jeff to be impressed. "I even had first-hand experience with grizzly bears."

"No shit! What's that all about?" Jeff was intrigued and instantly came to attention.

"They seemed to enjoy comin' into our camp for a time. When we made it unpleasant enough for them, they decided to move on."

"What did you do?", Jeff seemed interested.

"They wanted to raid our garbage, so we made sure what they dug out of it didn't agree with them." Deuce smiled as he remembered poisoning the bears. He still had some bearskin from those days. "The one we didn't poison," he paused to ask, "Did you ever have bear meat?" Again, Deuce wore a smirk on his face remembering his escapades.

"No. What do you do on the pipeline?" Jeff asked thinking it may be something he could do and no, he wasn't interested in eating bear meat.

"Whatever it took. Sometimes I would weld, help the welder, work the bending machine, and even do inspections. Over the past thirty years, I'd say I've done it all. Now that I'm gettin' ready to retire, I work as little as possible as a welder's helper."

"What kind of money do you make?" Appropriate or not, Jeff wanted to know.

"It depends on the job and who wins the contract. The range is normally eighteen to twenty-five per hour. The jobs we're doin' now, twenty-two." The wages kept deuce from pursuing his engineering degree when he was younger. He saw that he could make virtually the same amount of money welding on the pipeline. So, he opted not to waste his time or money for a piece of paper.

"If Jeff wanted to do something like that, what would he have to do?" Kathy thought the physical activity might be exactly what he needed.

Deuce knew he didn't want Jeff infiltrating his world at any level. He understood where Kathy was coming from, but there was no way he could allow it. Too many knew of his reputation with women. He didn't want his past to catch up with him in any way. "The first thing you have to do is take classes in weldin', all forms. Then you got to buy a book, which you get through the union. It normally costs four hundred dollars. Right now, they're not sellin' books, but it gives you time to get the classes out of the way." Deuce wanted to throw in as many obstacles as possible. "When they start sellin' the books again, and I can find out who you would have to go through to get one, seein' you're in Pennsylvania, I'll let you know."

"When do you think they'll start selling books again?" Jeff asked, unsure what the books were about.

"I'm not sure. Maybe the beginin' of the year. Everything depends on job availabilities, retirements, and deaths." A shiver went up his back when he said the word death, and he liked it.

"Jeff, they have classes at Penn Tech. Why don't you find out about them tomorrow?" Kathy hoped he was seriously thinking of welding, even if he didn't work on the pipeline. He needed to get some type of vocation. Working at a department store as a cashier was far from a career, and no way to support he would never be able to support himself.

"There's an idea," Deuce said in support. "Maybe by the time you graduate, a job opening will be available." He hoped it was in some other field, however.

The meal ended after numerous stories of working on the pipeline and accidents that could have been avoided. With each of the accidents, Deuce claimed to have warned them, but the foremen refused to listen. Over and over he stated, "What's right is right. What's wrong is wrong." Such an ambiguous statement for how he lived his life.

Ames Department Store was in the same area as Bonanza, at the Buckhorn Plaza. Within minutes Jeff was dropped off at the front door. Kathy found an open parking space near the front door, which she considered to be a good omen. Since she was there, and with the urging of Deuce, Kathy decided to look at the sale items she had been watching. Her finances were limited but looking didn't cost anything. She still felt a pang when she had to turn away from a good deal.

"Glad you decided to go in Kathy, I need to take care of a few things. All my toiletries need replaced; from soap to shaving cream. I would have picked them up on the way back home, but those little stores are outrageously priced. This kills two birds with one stone." Again, the shiver. Deuce had to get a container of deodorant. Old Spice was necessary to keep from offending anybody. Especially Kathy and the new challenges that laid ahead of him.

Hand in hand, Kathy and Deuce walked through the store. Kathy felt apprehensive being seen walking with another man. She worried about running into Carl or one of his family members, or one of his friends. She knew she wasn't to blame for his walking out, but she still felt guilty. *Please God, I committed adultery,* she thought in that instance. *Please, please don't let me run into anyone I know.*

As they passed the jewelry area, Kathy paused to look at the earrings she had wanted. They caught her eyes weeks ago, when she had been shopping. Regularly forty dollars, they were marked down to fifteen. Ruby, single-strand, dangle. She wanted them, but rent and mortgage were due. It seemed to be another omen. Over the intercom, they heard the store announce they would be closing in the next week.

"Do you like them?" Deuce leaned to see which hearings she was looking at.

"I've been watching them. They started at $40 and I wanted to see what they were now. Kathy knew what he was thinking, or afraid of what he was thinking. She added, "I think they're at the best price I'll get. Since they are down to $15, It's time to get them before anyone else." Kathy motioned for the clerk as she pulled a twenty-dollar bill from her pocket.

"Put that away." Deuce's authoritarianism just showed itself and he realized. *Stand down Sargent*! He demanded of himself.

By then, Kathy, shaken by his tone, instinctively responded, "I don't think so. I won't let any man by me jewelry again." The pangs in her stomach started again as she stood up for herself. *I hope that shit doesn't happen again.* She thought then quickly added, "But thanks."

"Sorry 'bout that. It's just a habit, wantin' to help." He had to make it work. He knew, too much too soon, was never successful. He had to pull in the reins.

Believing she had jumped to conclusions, Kathy apologized. "No, it's just the way I am. It's nothing to do with you." she said, "Besides, you've been buying stuff all along. I can take care of my own things. Do you know what I mean?"

"I hear that. Most women want the man to pay for everything, including jewelry. But paying for dinner, that's the way I was raised." Deuce hoped that explanation eased his premature display of domination.

The mood softened and they resumed their small talk. Kathy was satisfied with his explanation and kicked herself for assuming. Trust would be difficult; her wall was high. *The third is a charm.* She knew this was a fallacy. As far as she was concerned, there never would be a third; she vowed never to get married again. When it came to having a long-term relationship, she was leery. She was fearful of any man's ulterior motive, and there always was one. She knew this all too well, and was trying to keep it in check.

Chapter 12

The Run In

Returning home, Kathy noticed Carl's truck in the driveway. Fear struck her. She didn't need a confrontation between Deuce and Carl. "Shit!"

"What? Is that Carl's truck?" Deuce knew. Kathy had mentioned his black truck in passing. He had been watching for the truck in case he was a psycho. He didn't want to start anything so he wasn't worried about confrontation, and he didn't want to hurt him in front of Kathy. He would though, even if he was as big as she said. He had been trained in hand-to-hand combat, and had used it enough to call himself an expert. The only time he had ever been on the down side of the fight was as a teenager against his father. From that point forward he never lost a fight. Even at his age, most knew he could never be taken down in a hand-to-hand fight.

"Yeah. I hate to say this, but I need you to leave for a while. He's probably there to pick up a few things, and I want to be there to be sure he doesn't take anything he's not supposed to." Kathy's voice rang with anxiety. Her heart began to palpitate. She knew she would have to face him again, but why now? *Figures, meet someone and Carl's right there to fuck it up!*

"Are you sure you'll be okay? I can stay close by if you need me to. Would he hit you? Had he ever?" Deuce saw his plan in jeopardy. He'd hate to have to take him out to get what he wanted, but it wasn't out of the question. No one would know what happened to him. It's been done before, it can be done again. For some reason, when an adult goes missing without any evidence of foul play, the search didn't last long, and he counted on that.

"I think it will be okay. Anything he needs to say at this point doesn't matter. If you want to go back to the Lake, you can. It should only take a half hour." She preferred no confrontations.

"How you gonna get me to the car? He knows I'm here." Deuce asked.

"No, he knows there is a white car in the driveway. As far as he knows, it's a friend from work." Kathy answered.

"What I will do is go back to the bar I found earlier and have a beer. I will be sure I'm back in a half hour though. You'd better be here and okay. If not, I'll come looking for you!" And he meant it! He knew she was the one meant for him and he wouldn't let her go.

My God, he really cares. He doesn't even know me that well. Kathy felt something just then, but wasn't sure what; fear for the impending meeting with Carl or was it just, "*The Knight in Shining Armor,*" fantasy. She had felt so alone for so long, and Carl never filled that void. "I'll be here and fine. If his truck is still here when you come back, don't hesitate to come up to the door. He will not control anything in my life, especially my relationships."

"I like the sound of that, relationship. Haven't had one of them for a long time. Now that I've found you, I'm not wantin' to give that up." As Kathy's car came to a halt behind Carl's truck, Deuce pulled Kathy to him for a quick kiss, as he rubbed her right breast. "I'll be back," he said like Arnold Schwarzenegger with a southern drawl.

He slowly left her car for his. As Kathy hoped, Carl failed to hear her pulling into the driveway. Deuce seemed to walk slowly without care, as if to say, *come on, try me.* Kathy loved his slow confident movement, but it also added to her anxiety. She watched as he backed his car out of the driveway and pulled away. After he pulled away, she took his spot and quickly got out. As she walked up the steps to the front door, Carl opened it with a glare she had never seen before. *Here we go.* Kathy prepared herself mentally for his well-known bullshit.

"Whose car was that in the driveway?" He asked with a suspicious tone.

"A friend of mine. Why? And why is it any of your business? I should ask you why your truck is in my driveway?" Kathy wasn't having any of his attitude.

"This is still in my name too!" He said referring to the mobile home. "So, I have the right to be here."

"No, not anymore. You walked out over a month ago, without any contact till now. That's called abandonment. In fact, I want you to give me the key so I won't have to worry about you coming in some night while I am away." Kathy was so ready to move on, she didn't want to worry about Carl walking in on her and Deuce. Carl was passive aggressive to the point of being explosive.

"When I have all my shit out of here, you'll get the key." Carl stood blocking the door with the two dogs wagging their tails, trying to get to Kathy. "You find yourself a piece of ass? Is that why you want the keys?""

"Just get what you came to get, and get out. You leave me your key or I'll have the locks changed by the end of the night. The next time you need something, make an appointment." Kathy pulled the screen door open and pushed past him.

"Well you will have change them, cause I'm keeping them. I'm taking Rufus with me."

A sense of loss came over Kathy. She never considered losing Rufus. He was her protector. She trained him for when she gained use of her legs again. Her M.S. was the relapsing and remitting type. Legally, he was her Service Dog, but he was also bought as Carl's dog. Carl found him at a benefit for the S.P.C.A. while he was hanging with his friends playing softball. Kathy would never stand in his way. She would miss him deeply. Bea, however, was Jeff's dog, so she knew he wouldn't take her. "What else do you want?" she asked abruptly, seeing two garbage bags full.

"I got the rest of my clothes, but I still need to get the rest of my tools."

"Well, get them!" Kathy felt her blood pressure rising. "Anything else?" She walked to the kitchen and placed her bag on the table. Turning around and leaning on the table, she saw Carl standing at the front door with a disgruntled look.

"Don't you want to know where I am living?" Carl called as he was leaving.

"Nope. Just make sure you change your address." Turning abruptly, Kathy entered her room, slamming the door behind her. Throwing herself onto the bed, tears filled her eyes. "Why did he have to come back like that," she sobbed. *That bastard has the audacity to think he can show up whenever he wants. I'll be surprised if Deuce even comers back. He probably thinks I want him back. If I don't see the key on the table when he leaves, I swear I'm changing the locks!*

Kathy remained in the bedroom listening for Carl to leave. It seemed to take forever. With each passing moment, the fear a possible confrontation if Deuce came back too soon. Her anxiety peaked. A wave of nausea got her attention. Before she knew it, she found herself racing to the bathroom to throw-up.

Finally, Kathy heard the door slam with a crash. The picture next to the door came down shattering glass about the hallway. She gathered herself up and walked out through the bedroom door to find Bea the in front of it as though she needed consolation. Rufus was the gone, along with his leash. She listened as she heard his truck peel out of the driveway. Moments later, she heard Deuce pull in. *He and,* she thought in that instance. *I wonder if Carl got a look at him. I'm moving on, you son of a bitch!*

Passing by the table, Kathy noticed he left the key. *Thank God.* Kathy proceeded to open the door with a sigh. Just as she opened it Deuce stood ready to knock. "You must have passed him, Carl just left."

"No, to be honest, I parked up the road there. You don't know how I wish you'd have let me in. I was worried sick." Deuce noticed that Kathy was crying. "Did he hurt you?"

"No, I just lost it after he said he was taking Rufus."

"I saw that. Do you want me to get him back?" Deuce made an empty offer. He was glad there was only one dog to worry about now.

"No, it was his dog anyways. I still have Bea, although she belongs to Jeff."

Deuce pulled Kathy into his arms, wrapping them tightly around her as she laid her head on his shoulder. "Baby, are you sure? I hate seein' you hurting like this."

"Deuce, I'm just glad he's gone." Kathy pulled the bottle of wine from the fridge wanting to wash away the pain. Deuce however, took it away from her.

"Let me open that for you. Grab me a beer." He was more than happy to allow her to forget her problems. He thought about grabbing the moonshine from the car, but he knew he would need to conserve it for the future. He opened the wine as Kathy pulled two glasses from her cabinet.

"Well, there's one good thing that happened; Carl left the house key. I told him if he needed anything else, he had to call for an appointment." Kathy held her glass as Deuce filled it with burgundy wine. Without hesitation, she took a large swallow.

"Whoa, slow down." Deuce had something special to share with her today. He hoped she wouldn't mind. Pulling a rolled-up plastic bag from his pocket, he took his chance. "Besides, this might be a little better than wine." He proceeded to unwrap the bag to show its contents. "Smell this," He said holding it under her nose.

"It's marijuana. Do you smoke?" Deuce figured most everyone had at least tried it once and hoped she would be willing to partake.

"I haven't smoked in a long time. Roll it up. I'm ready." Kathy hadn't been exposed to marijuana since the 90's. And today she would be glad for the chance to try it again.

"Girl after my own heart." He said as he pulled a pack of paper from his pocket. "Didn't think I did anything like that, did you?"

He had smoked and grown weed most of his life. With random drug testing, he had to be sure he kept his system clear of THC. If there were no job accidents

while he was working, he wouldn't be tested. This was one reason he refused to work in unsafe conditions. Within minutes, Deuce and Kathy sat at the table sipping their drinks, smoking the joint. The THC was potent in the marijuana and

Kathy felt it after three tokes. She had forgotten what the high felt like, and enjoyed the euphoria. They smoked until the first burn of the fingers.

"Did you know that marijuana is West Virginia's number one cash crop?" Deuce said boastfully. "Granny Rose use to tend my garden while I was on the road workin'. She'd pull it in and hang it in the barn to dry. By the time I came home, I'd find a barn full. Take 'bout a good month to dry in the barn, but once I had it bagged up, I got rid of it with it within a week." Deuce smiled as he reminisced.

"How long ago was that?" Kathy thought it happened back in the 70's.

"Granny Rose died in the late 80s, so I'd say it's been about 10 years since I grew it like that. Sure was profitable." Deuce thought about getting it started again as soon as he retired. He had the perfect place for it. A simple farm on top of a mountain with one way in and one way out. A dog protected it while he was gone, so when it was time to plant, there would always be a guard on duty.

"Let me tell you, I haven't smoked it for at least five years, and that was at a family picnic where my brother shared it with me. So, you know it wasn't much." Kathy wished she didn't have all the drama around, but paranoia was a strong side effect. She had studied its side effects, knowing her son would most likely try it and found there were no deaths attributed to marijuana.

"I wanted to show this to you earlier, but I was scare't. And I'm not scare't of anything. You could have been dead against it. And I'd left it behind." He said this knowing he wasn't going anywhere. If Kathy would have been against the marijuana, he would have saved it for when she was back in West Virginia with him. Then there would be no choice.

"It's no big deal," Kathy assured him. She knew she had to avoid it while she was working, but he wasn't around during the week, so she little reason to worry. She always enjoyed the buzz, and since she wasn't a drinker, *A little weed occasionally couldn't hurt.*

Deuce pulled Kathy to his lips. He was relieved this obstacle was out of the way. He felt Kathy relax in his arms. "Let's finish this wine in the bedroom."

Stretching out on the bed felt wonderful. Kathy knew it was for more than sleeping, but coming from the uncomfortable bed at the Lodge, her queen-size, quilt top mattress would enhance what was to come. The last time the bed had experienced the activity of sex was a very long time ago. It was time to break it in again. Kathy was the first to stand. "Let me lock the door." She said as she quickly walked to the front door. Kathy trembled inside. In her eyes this was a big step. Deuce would be the first man since Carl to be in her bed. Without another word, Kathy walked past Deuce, grabbed his hand, and led him to the bedroom.

It took little time to remove their clothes. In a matter of seconds the two were engulfed in each other's passion. Kathy clung desperately to him, as Deuce slipped in and without consideration to his surroundings. Kathy became aware of his "absence in the moment," and stopped him in mid-motion, forcing him to take a passive role by laying on his back. Deuce complied wholeheartedly. Kathy kissed him with forcefulness as she placed him inside her. She needed the control this time. Her life had spun so out of control, she at least needed control over her own pleasure and Deuce was more than happy to give in and bask in his own success. She freed herself to experience many positions with Deuce during passion play.

Deuce held on for as long as he could. He wanted to wait for Kathy, but he could no longer hold out and exploded with pure pleasure. Kathy, filled with pleasure, rolled him to the side and burrowed into his chest.

"That was great!" Kathy moaned from his chest and cavern. As he held her tightly in his in his arms, Kathy started to feel more at ease. He continued to be tender and respectful at every turn; something she had always wanted. She was infatuated.

Deuce, basking in his brilliance, could only think, *she might be the one who lasts the longest. She certainly isn't as shy as Cindy, or as mouthy as Maggie. Oh, the pleasure that awaits.* Verbally deuce replied, "yes you were." Yet, Deuce continued to fantasize.

When the evening ended, Deuce made sure to get Kathy's phone number, knowing he needed to keep in touch, to carry out his plans. If all goes well he hoped to have her headed to West Virginia by the first of the month. He wasn't going to wait much longer. Come hell or high water, she was going to be his.

Chapter 13

Confrontation

The house was quiet after Deuce left. Kathy sat motionlessly on the couch, in silence, her only entertainment was her thoughts. Racing at first, but soon focused on Deuce. Her stomach reacted as she fantasized about West Virginia. Suddenly her thoughts switched to John Denver, *"Take me home, Country Roads, to the place I belong. West Virginia, mountain mama. Take me home country road."* Kathy reminisced about her high school years when this song and John Denver played a key role in her life. One of her treasured forty-fives was his 1971 single, *"Take me Home, Country Road"*. Kathy would listen to songs from "Grandma's feather Bed" to "Sunshine on My Shoulders" on her small turntable until her siblings would complain about the sound.

Kathy shook her head, realizing quickly that she needed to pull herself together and get back to the task at hand. The empty bottle, buried under the trash; check. The makeshift ashtray with two roaches and eight cigarette butts was cleaned and put back under her plant; check and check. She was saving those roaches though. Jeff need not know what happened there; but Kathy would never forget. Too many coincidences have happened in the presence of Deuce. She always connected coincidences with God. She saw the omens. She felt the love. Her beliefs came together today. She couldn't deny it.

It wasn't quite nine when the phone rang. "Hello?" *Who could be calling me now?*

"Hey beautiful, you miss me?" Deuce took little time to call her. He wanted his voice to be the last one she heard that night.

"Not yet; I need to get a shower and get in bed first."

"What'cha wearing?" Deuce added.

"Close your eyes; remember what I had on when you left? BINGO! Sexy huh?" Still waiting to shower, Kathy wasn't interested in games. "I bet you have on the same clothes too. Am I wrong, or right?"

"Wrong! I took my pants off. I will end up taking my shirt off too. I sleep nude. Clothes get in the way. Is there somebody else missing you tonight?" Deuce inquired. Even though he had doubts, beautiful Kathy couldn't have other suitors. *Granny Rose knows how to pick them*! He thought.

"Is that a joke? What? You think I'm a slut? Didn't I tell you Carl left one month ago? Shit, you're my first since." A doubt bloomed in Kathy's psyche. Controller? A doubter? Or is he playing a game to pass the time? "I'm surprised you called me this soon."

"Did you want me to wait 'til tomorrow? I'll hang up and do that." Deuce hoped she wanted to talk a little longer.

"No, I'm just not use to the attention." Kathy softened her tone.

"Well sweetheart, you better get used to it now. I'm not letting you forget me." Deuce was calling from a phone next to his bed, giving him access to himself as needed. Tonight, was one of those nights. Even with the satisfaction earlier, his hand was drawn to his member. Stroking it slowly as he talked to Kathy, remembering the day. "I just wanted to ask you if you were available this weekend?"

"Available? Hell, I haven't even started to plan for tomorrow Why?" What was Deuce thinking?

"I've got something planned if you're interested." He said cautiously.

"What?" Kathy perked up. Hmm a mystery. She wanted to see him again, but what was so important? "Sounds like a mystery. Let me tell you, tentatively yes. Kathy held back from giving a definite commitment. With the sudden appearance of Carl, she worried about further trouble. "If it all goes well at work, no problem. But, Jeff has to keep the car so he can get to work." Kathy added.

"It's for me to know, and you to be surprised." Deuce knew his plan continued to work. Up to this point, she trusted him. Hopefully it would continue. *Bwa ha ha, into my clutches*, The Snidely Whiplash memory took over. *After we get there, she'll see the mystery; there is no return trip to PA.*

Kathy paused to deliberate. *I've got to learn to trust. Yet, he never gave me a reason to mistrust. I want to be with him.* "When do we leave?" Kathy responded with an unforeseen glee.

"Sounds like a plan. I'll call ya' Thursday to remind you. We gotta leave 'bout 7 o'clock. You off work by then?" Deuce wanted to leave before the eight o'clock traffic. *Seven hours on the road gets us in 'bout two A.M.* Surprise had worked before, Deuce wasn't worried. But using entrapment as a surprise had never been tried. Now he would use his engineering knowledge to gear-up his plan. *She will be mine; there's no doubt!*

"**POUND, POUND, POUND!** "Hey there is someone at the door." **POUND, POUND, POUND!** "Let me call you Wednesday."

"Sounds like someone wants in. Do you want me to stay on the phone and make sure you're okay?" Deuce heard someone eager to get in the door. For once his heart dropped from fear; and not for the possible wrench in his plan. He sat up ready to drive to the rescue. Grabbing his jeans, he pulled them on.

"It'll be ok. If you want to call me back later, I'll fill you in. Carl probably forgot something." The pounding continued. "Talk to you later okay?" Kathy's agitation grew with each **POUND**.

"I'll call you in a few minutes. If you need me, I'm here." Hating to end the call, Deuce hung up. *Better not be her ex causing problems. He'd suddenly disappear. He isn't going to ruin my plans.*

Kathy hung up the phone, trembling inside as she walked to the door. "I'm coming!" She called. Looking out the small window on the door, Carl stared back. She opened the door with trepidation.

"What the fuck took you so long?" he bellowed as the door opened. Without hesitation, he pushed his way past Kathy, nearly knocking her off her feet. "You had that guy here for a long time. What were you doing? Fucking him? Slut! You been seeing him long?" Carl's anger was apparent from the vein protruding from his forehead.

"Who the hell do you think you are? And who put you in charge? You left! So, what makes you think you can show up again and start problems? You have no right to be here, let alone question me about anything!" Kathy hated his outrage. She always felt like she had to walk on egg-shells around his passive aggressive ways. Tonight, she would stand her ground.

"I have every right to be here. My name is on the title and mortgage. Until it's sold I can come in here any time I want." Carl hadn't thought of that before he gave up the key. But, after talking to his mom and stepfather, he wanted to exert his right. He stomped to the table looking for the key, and slammed his hand where he had placed it. "Where the hell is my key?! You better not have given it to your boyfriend!"

"You're not getting it back Carl, according to the law," Kathy recanted. "You abandoned me along with the home. I talked to a lawyer today. You can only have your personal items. You are more than welcome to them, just call first. No matter what you were told, you cannot be here whenever you want." Kathy hadn't talked to a lawyer, but to her supervisor at her office.

"You're more of a bitch then I remember! If you want to play hardball, I'll see you in court! Until then, you better not keep me from getting my things." Carl kept getting increasingly agitated. He knew he was in the wrong since walking out, but, *I'll be damned if she gets everything.* Before he left, Carl needed one more thing, his prize collection, his prize possessions. He hoped they were still there.

"As soon as you get what you came for, I want you to leave. AND, don't come by here again without calling first. By the way, in case you give a shit, Jeff is taking this hard. He's blaming me for you walking out, and he's being real belligerent towards me. I'm sick of taking the blame. Why don't you take Jeff and talk with him?" None the less, Kathy knew when Carl held a grudge, it was written in stone. The sad part was; the psychological damage was already done.

Kathy retreated to her room with the portable phone in tow. When Deuce returned her call, she wanted to pick it up right away. Hopefully

Carl would be gone by then. Gathering his "prize" collection of baseball cards was the reason for his return. Family didn't even rate a second place. So, there was no surprise when Jeff took over his "position in the home" with his anger. To have a chance with a loving relationship was the relief she needed.

Deuce, hearing the pounding at the door, debated whether to go back now or wait. He heard the stress in her voice. He correctly assumed it was Carl at the door. If that son-of-a-bitch lays a hand on her, he's dead! He refused to have his plan interrupted. *Maybe I need to speed things up! I don't need that EX coming between us. She is the one who will share my desires. And I know she is the one who will last. She has enough weight, nice size breasts, and a tight pussy! When she said only 150 times in twelve years, she was telling the truth! How lucky can I get? Those planets sure are good to me*! Sweat started to pour down his face as he thought of what was to come. He had waited three long years for another chance to make Granny Rose proud. She never liked easy, money hungry, women. And if Kathy came with him willingly, he knew she was the one. He knew she couldn't be attracted to him for his looks, so it had to be due to the lies he told her. *She thinks I have a farm and gas wells. Ha! Gets them every time. I might have a home, but it isn't what she thinks. I do know one thing, I must get the place ready before I get her there. After she's there, there's no coming back.* Deuce returned to the bar and ordered a beer with a chaser of Black Label Jack Daniel from New. She was prompt when she saw that $100 bill laying on the bar. "Keep the change."

"Deuce, why? Shit, that could buy you drinks for the next two days! What are you so stressed about? You're sweating like a steer. Are you feeling okay? Should I call an ambulance?" New saw a sweaty man giving away money like he was repenting before he dies.

"Not stressed, just waiting. I have a call to make, and hope she say yes." He was hopeful she'd jump at the chance to visit West Virginia.

"Jesus Deuce! You didn't!" New's chin hit the floor. *Bitch! Fucking user! Money hungry slut*! New turned, grabbing the Jack Daniels, a larger than normal glass, and poured a triple shot. On the other side, she poured herself a ½ shot. Turning around, she proudly displayed the two drinks. "To the Newlyweds!" She announced to the bar. The three old timers shrugged and went back to drinking. The only two couples left in the bar watched with knowing smiles.

"What? Fuck that! I was talking about taking a trip! What the fuck?" He was taken aback at the conclusion she'd made.

"Damn, I'm sorry. I know your team is due to leave soon I would've married you, given the chance. I fucked up." She held the shot up as an apology turned toast. "Let toast to an apology. To the man with a plan, and those that are blind!" New slammed the ½ shot more aware of the burn. *Penitence! Catholic Girl Gone Wild!* she thought.

Deuce raised his glass high and toasted the last part the strongest. "Nothing like three blind mice. Keeping them that way was the challenge. "Golly gee Miss Maggie, that'll put hair on my chest! New, you always know what I need." Then his thoughts went to Kathy. *I'll give her five more minutes,* he thought. *I'll kill him if he causes problems. By the way it looks, he's already messed Kathy's life up. I don't want him fucking it up for me.* Deuce smiled at New.

"Now that's what I'm talking about! You saw that coming and you knew it would work. Still need that yes?" New hovered close to solidify their relationship. Not only was he respectful, she loved the tips. But the sudden flash of that hundred-dollar bill worried her. In all her years of bartending, she had never known anyone as nice as Deuce. It was funny how she worried about him as if he was her brother.

Chapter 14

Or beg him to come back.

Kathy was happy to see Carl leave. Jeff would be home soon and she was glad the interaction between the two was avoided. She wasn't sure if Jeff would have exploded, either way, she didn't want to see it. Anxious for Deuce's call, she felt a sigh of relief. *Deuce won't be around long anyways, but I won't let Carl fuck it up!*

Kathy heard footsteps on her deck. Her heart started racing in fear of another confrontation with Carl. She watched as the doorknob turned and the door flung open with force. She held her breath. There in the doorway stood Jeff. Kathy breathed a sigh of relief.

"Hey mom, did you get anything at Ames while you were there with Deuce?" Kathy knew he hoped she had gotten something for him.

"I got those earrings I'd been watching for a while." Kathy's heart began to slow as she began to realize the worst was over with Carl. "How was work?"

"It was work." Jeff responded nonchalantly. "Did you call Dad?"

"No need, he came by tonight for more of his stuff." That was one confrontation she was glad to be over.

"What did he say about me? Did you tell him about Ames? This had been a painful subject between Jeff and Carl since he was sixteen. Before Carl checked out of his life, Jeff had promised to find a job.

"I told him you were working at Ames."

"But did he ask?" Jeff really hoped so.

"Jeff, he was more interested in getting his prize possessions, than how we were doing. You should know that by now."

"You started bitching at him, didn't you! That's why he didn't ask." Jeff's temper was starting to flair. Jeff wasn't sure how he felt. Was he angrier at his mom or his dad? Deep down he knew his mom was telling the truth. "If I see him…" With a deep breath, "I'm going to tell him…" With an angry grumble, Jeff turned and stormed to his bedroom.

"JEFF, I DIDN'T SAY ANYTHING!" Kathy called out as he disappeared. *Damn, it wasn't enough to just "abandon" me? I don't understand why he abandoned Jeff. Why do men not see it? Are they all self-centered?* Tears began flowing down her cheeks.

The phone interrupted Kathy's anguish. *Just in time*! Grabbing the portable phone, Kathy retreated to her bedroom. "Hello?"

"Hey Baby! Miss me?" The deep southern voice, familiar to her heart, spoke softly and seductively.

"Deuce!" an instant smile covered her face. She felt her shoulders release.

"You 'specting someone else to call you Baby?" Deuce teased.

"Not with a southern drawl like yours." Kathy wanted to rebut his tease. "If you only knew

how glad I am you called!"

"Glad enough to come down and see me tonight?" Deuce knew it wasn't possible since she worked in the morning.

"You know I can't. Why don't you come up here?!" Kathy knew he had to work in the morning, but she would have loved his company again.

"Okay, I will." Just what she wanted to hear.

Flabbergasted, Kathy wasn't sure how to react. "Really?"

Deuce was shocked she even offered. Even though it wasn't feasible, Deuce decided to have a little fun with her. "Well, it only took 25 minutes to get home; I need to grab some things for tomorrow and I'll head your way. He smirked at his vision of a "deer in the headlights" look on her face.

Kathy was stunned. So stunned she couldn't reply.

"Hello? You still there?" Deuce knew he would get her goat.

Kathy tried to figure out a comeback. She knew it wouldn't go over well with Jeff. She also knew she wouldn't get any sleep. "You know, now that I think about it, you and I wouldn't get any sleep. But I'll take you up on that offer on Friday or Saturday night."

"Come to think of it, you're probably right." Deuce wanted to let her off the hook. "Besides, we are leaving for the weekend anyways."

Kathy smiled. She knew he let her off easy. With Jeff's abandonment issues flaring up, "I'm glad. So, where we going again?" *Perfect timing*, she thought.

"Aren't you a sly one. Don't trust me? You know I was just joshing you, don't you? But we're still going, aren't we?" Deuce saw a flash of distress. "You know I'd never hurt you." *Get a yes, get a yes.* Deuce needed another yes.

"May I ask you something first?" Kathy couldn't believe this was happening.

"Anything my dear." He wasn't sure what was coming next.

"Where have you been all my life?" She'd finally found the one!

"Looking for you." He replied. Bingo! My plan is right on schedule.

Chapter 15

Doubt Seeps In

Monday morning Kathy began her routine. Coffee to wake her up; a dress for her job, (Black silk style shoestring dress with a black and white short jacket). Kathy began her 50-mile trek to work. She loved the length of time it took to get to work. While the music played, she planned her day.

She had a family to present an insurance plan to for their baby girl. Another family for Life Insurance for the father, who was a self-employed Farmer. Insurance premiums to collect. Then, spend the rest of the day cold calling.

Instead, Kathy reminisced. *I never thought I'd meet a man like him. His stories intrigue me. If I could have dreamed him into existence, I could never have dreamed this well. I love the deep southern drawl and his West Virginian dialect.* Kathy was enamored by how he made her feel. Then, "Lady" by Kenny Rogers began to play on her radio. Turning it up, she sang along.

The song continued, as Kathy related the song's lyrics to her relationship with Deuce. Obsession began to take root. Fantasy and reality slowly began to blur. Kathy had been isolated from true love for so long, she began to equate infatuation with love. Even with her degree in Psychology, Kathy was so desperate for love, she failed to look at her relationship from a third-party perspective. This was a mistake she would never forget.

Her day proceeded as planned, occasionally getting lost in her thoughts. With Deuce seeping into her every thought, Kathy was glad to have written all her daily plans on paper. Then came a detour. Kathy found herself driving through Benton looking for the "warehouse" Deuce told her about. This was the meeting place for the workers before and after work. She believed it was something large, so it would be easy to find. It was a trailer surrounded by equipment, cars, and dirt. When she had driven three miles outside of Benton, there were fewer houses, and buildings became sparse. She gave up, turned around, and began to drive home dejected. She tried hard not to follow her heart, but the pangs in her stomach steered her towards the lake.

Deuce, I hope to God you were telling me the truth about your job. Kathy worried he had just told her whatever it took to get her in bed. *But that Mike said the same thing about their job.* Kathy slowed as she passed the trailer again, looking for a car like Deuce's. There was none. She drove on towards the lake. *I'll stop at the Lodge first and see if his car is there,* Kathy thought. *And if not, I'll go to Shari's and check later.* The obsession began to grow with every passing moment and still Kathy was oblivious to it.

With a right turn, Kathy was headed towards the lake. She increased the radio volume when Alan Jackson sang, "Tall, Tall Trees and All the Waters in the Seas, I'm a Fool, Fool, Fool for You." She floated in her own dream world of love, as the song played she saw Deuce's face. She was beginning to see Deuce as her soulmate. Deuce was everything she wanted in a man.

As Kathy returned to reality, she saw a white car in front of her, which seemed to be traveling towards the lake. With a second look, she saw the familiar dew rag. Her heart started to race as a smile of recognition came over her face. Excited, she started honking the horn to get his attention. he was stopped at an intersection on Beaver Lake Road.

Fucking Idiots! Deuce had already had to put up with Tibble all day. He was one of the welders that most helpers despised. Deuce had volunteered to work with him today to avoid a lay-off and stick around until his plan had come together. Tibble however, had pissed him off so bad, he took off early to preserve his composure. Now with this asshole behind him, pissing him off, he thought he might have to take out his aggression on him. He turned his signal on after he turned towards the lake, pulled to the side of the road for the confrontation. Looking up, he saw a red Saturn doing the same thing. He was wrapped so tight, he failed to recognize the car, threw his in park, and jumped out ready to tear the driver a new one.

When Kathy saw how quickly he pulled over, her heart skipped a beat. *It must be a sign. I needed to see him so bad!* she though as she opened the door and he stepped out.

Deuce saw the door swing open and braced himself for a confrontation. As his eyes focused on the thin bare legs in black pumps stepping out of the car, his inflated blood pressure dropped as he saw the red-head emerge from the driver's seat. "Baby!" This was all he could say as a smile took the place of his anger.

Kathy was smiling at the sound of his voice. She bolted toward him eager to feel his arms around her. She saw the dirt clinging to him from his long day at work, but refused to allow it to inhibit their embrace. Without uttering a word, she embedded herself in his arms and kissed him deeply. For a moment, she was lost in her own fantasy of her southern gentleman.

"Good thing it was you," Deuce said as he continued to embrace her. "After the day I had, I was ready to tear the idiot honking apart. You made my day!"

"I tried to find you today after I finished work. I don't know what you've done to me, but I like it."

Deuce liked the sound of that. He didn't realize how well his plan was coming together. *It looks like I can move to the next step.* He reciprocated her grasp. "Do you have time to have dinner with me before you go home?"

Kathy hadn't even thought about eating all day. The offer of food made her realize how hungry she really was. "Sure. Where do you want to eat?"

"Might as well go to the Lodge. I'll get cleaned up and we'll go down to the bar and get somethin' to eat."

"Sounds good to me." Kathy looked down at her watch and saw it was after five. She thought about Jeff for just a moment and dismissed the guilt that tried to enter the picture. But Kathy had to remember, *I need to find my own happiness, like Jeff needs to find his. I just hope he finds his sooner than I found mine.*

Kathy knew when Deuce was done with his shower, there was more to come. Walking out of the shower, his towel fell to the floor as he approached her. Her shoes laid on the floor beside the bed where she was sitting and she knew, by the look in Deuce's eyes and the solid erection, her clothes were soon to follow.

"Ya know, I kinda like what you do to me." Deuce gave Kathy a slow smile.

Kathy knew what he was referring to, and patted the bed next to her. "So, what are you going to do about it?"

Deuce didn't hesitate and fell on top of her, reaching up her dress and through her underpants. His mouth encompassed hers with a kiss she liked, soft and passionate. Deuce felt her hand search and find him, stroking slow and hard. It only took a moment to remove her dress and bra, and a second to remove her under pants. He stroked her clit and inserted his finger, but wanted more from her this time. He pulled away.

"What's wrong?" Kathy was confused.

"I'm thinkin' we need to slow down a bit." Deuce watch as Kathy attempted to read between the lines. He watched as her blue eyes darted back and forth trying to figure him. *If she's thinkin' I'm pulling away, this ought to throw her for a loop.*

"What are you saying?" Kathy was bewildered.

"I'm not sure I'm ready to get my heart broken again. And you my dear could tear me up. I'm fallin' awful quick. You've only been separated a month. Who's to say I'm not just a rebound for you." Deuce stood and walked away from the bed. With a forlorn look on his face, he said. "You know what I'm sayin'?"

Kathy didn't know what to say. She hadn't even considered him as a rebound, but she understood what he was saying. She was aware he was working in the area for only a short time, but she was willing to accept that. Here he is, saying he is falling for her and to no surprise, she had already fallen for him. "Deuce, you saying you want to stop seeing me?"

"Well, if it were up to me, I'd take you home and never let you go. I just don't really know how you feel about me. Am I an affair for the time bein'? or we gonna pursue this?" Deuce put the ball in her court.

Kathy peered into Deuce's soft blue eyes. "Sweetheart, I want it to be something more. Here I am searching for you only one day after I met you. I can't stop thinking about you. I wonder if you're okay, thinking about me, and when I can see you again. I feel like a teenager with her first love. And yes, I'm falling in love with you too. Kathy patted the bed beside her again.

This was what Deuce was looking for. Her admission he had won her heart showed he was ready for the next step. He gladly responded to her call, laying her down with a prolonged kiss. Together they made love in celebration. He honored her admission with multiple orgasms.

The time flew by quickly and after they had eaten, like a gentleman, Deuce walked Kathy to her car. "You still up for this weekend?"

"Where did you say we were going? I've got to tell Jeff." She was hoping for a clue.

"When it comes closer. I just want it to be a surprise for now." Deuce smiled at her curiosity.

Kathy just reciprocated with a kiss. "I've got to get going. Jeff's probably wondering where I am. Give me a call tomorrow. I know I won't be able to come down again until Friday. But wait, are you going pick me up for the surprise?"

"Yeah. You might want to leave the car for Jeff to use while you're gone. I'll fill the tank for him."

"You won't have to; it will already be filled." Kathy could and would. She just hoped Jeff would be okay with it. Even if she had to endure his anger, she needed this and wanted it.

The two kissed and embraced one last time. Deuce held Kathy's door while she entered. Bending down for the victory kiss, he made sure it was deep enough for one last reaction.

Chapter 16

The Plan

How am I going to do this? Deuce thought as he watched Kathy drive away. *I'm gonna ask for a lay-off this Friday due to poor working conditions. They would be stupid to refuse me.* Deuce had to make his plan infallible. This was the weekend the plan would come together. He had Kathy right where he wanted her. Nothing would stop him now!

Granny, you see what I found?" He thought as he said a little prayer to his Granny Rose. *You always said I needed to find a fiery Redhead. Well I think this is her. I need to be careful. She could win my heart. She's not one of those money hungry bitches you told me about nor is she the slut you warned me about. And she's certainly not a crack whore like you thought most women were. Granny, she might be the one. I guess we'll find out soon enough. I guess if she doesn't put up too much fuss over the dungeon, I'll keep her.*

Deuce turned and walked into the Lodge. He grew to like this cozy secluded Inn. It had everything he needed. It had a comfortable room, a country setting, and a bar with a restaurant. And with Kathy as desert, Deuce couldn't ask for more.

"Betty, get me a Bud Light, will you?" Deuce asked the owner as she approached the bar.

"Deuce, what are you doing with that girl?" she asked as she placed the beer in front of him. "She seems awful young. You better watch your wallet."

Deuce's blood pressure began to rise. "What are you trying to say? She's only after me for the money?" He knew that was what she was trying to say and as far as he was concerned, she had no business being concerned. He knew she had tried to fix him up with her niece. *Maybe that's why she tried to get them together.*

"Well you never know. I'm just saying, you're too nice a guy to let someone take advantage of you." Betty knew she had to change the subject. "By the way, the Little League World Series will be starting soon, don't you?"

"Well Betty, I won't be here after this week, so you needn't worry. There's a layoff comin' at the end of the week. So, I'll be goin' home." Deuce was glad he made the decision before coming back to the Lodge. With that kind of attitude, Betty would have been a thorn in his side, and he didn't need that.

"So, this rent payment will be the last." Deuce reached into his pocket and pulled out $110 for the rest of the week. "Here," he said as he counted it out for her. Then he threw in an extra $50. "This is for you. Buy yourself something pretty." Deuce meant it facetiously, as he believed no matter what she bought herself, it would never help her personality.

Kathy's head was filled with curious thoughts. *It wouldn't be anything material, I hope. Could it* be a *dinner at a fancy restaurant? Maybe we're going somewhere special for the night.* He had mentioned something about the Pocono Mountains. *Wait...* Kathy's mind took an interesting turn. *He better not ask me...* "Damn!" She said out load. "I hate surprises."

The drive home took longer than expected. Traffic back-ups because of Amish carriages happened often during the summer months. Kathy noticed it was 7:56 pm on the dashboard and realized her mind was obsessing over Deuce. "Insurance!" she exclaimed as she came back to reality.

Kathy never thought her career would end up like this. Peddling insurance with a degree in Psychology and Education. Her hope had been to become a School Counselor. Her only job possibilities ended with; "maybe the School District will call," to "at least you have a job.

Two hundred eighty per dollars per week certainly beat that possibility any day.

Deuce pulled in to Larry's Inn. He spotted a truck filled with welding equipment, and knew Mike was in the bar. He hadn't hooked up with him since meeting Kathy. He needed a chance to grab a couple of those pills for his trip home. There was never any question, and he always compensated Mike for all.

Chapter 17

Anxiety Takes Its Toll

Damn I'm so tired of this. It was Thursday night and the only policy sold today was a Life insurance policy for a baby. The parents took advantage of a grow-up policy, freeing the child of high premiums for the first 25 years. This was great for the child, but a low commission for the agent. Kathy's pocket money was dwindling, so she chose to forgo lunch and put her pocket change toward gasoline.

I don't understand why Deuce hasn't called. Did he change his mind and not tell me? Kathy was perplexed. *I thought we had plans.* Kathy had tried calling him numerous times. First his room, then the bar. Betty, the owner, had promised to tell him she called. After a while she left it up to him to call her. Her trip home seemed endless. Fifty miles to work ended up being ninety. Music became her only driving companion. Pessimism seeped into her pores. Interstate 80 and her cruise control, enabled her to lean back in her seat back to a more comfortable position. Country music soothed her.

The day had been long and hot. The "Q", north central PA's number one country music station, as they called themselves played the next song; Garth Brooks', *If Tomorrow Never Comes.* Kathy perked up immediately. She loved Garth Brooks, then without hesitation, she turned the radio off. *He just used me! Wanted a piece of ass and there I was! Surprise! You won't be hearing from me again! Fuck men! I thought he was something special. Come to find out, He was that special asshole I'd seen before.* Kathy pounded the steering wheel. "Damn! Why me? Do

I have a sign on my forehead: Pick me, the asshole here!" Kathy yelled into thin air while tears spontaneously began flowing down her cheeks. Her obsessive thoughts became self-destructive.

By the time Kathy pulled into her driveway, she went from thinking Deuce was an asshole to he'd probably been working late. Then her thoughts jumped to: he was killed on the job, and no one would call her. A pit grew heavier in her stomach. Back and forth between love and hate. No matter her feelings, she felt as if she was drowning in them. Any obsessive thought, with no rhyme nor reason, was one of the most helpless feelings anyone could experience.

Kathy walked up to her door dejected. *Tomorrow is Friday; Payday, yeah.* Kathy saw no light at the end of her dark damp tunnel. It was after six by the time she got home. Jeff was nowhere around, so Kathy assumed he was at work. Bea waited for Kathy at the front door wagging her tail, jumping up for attention. Forgetting her woes for the moment, Kathy stooped to let Bea slobber her kisses around her face. "Bea! My baby! I love you too." This was the most enjoyable moment of her day. Unconditional love was all she needed, both her and Bea. *Maybe I am meant to be a Dog Lady!*

"Stop, stop!" Kathy laughed and pushed Bea away.

"She's happy to see you." A voice emanating from the direction of Jeff's room, startled her.

"Don't you work tonight?" She asked.

"Nope. I made dinner though. Yours is in the microwave. I didn't know when you were getting home and I'm going out with my friends tonight. I was getting ready to leave a note. Now I won't have to." He was relieved she came home.

Kathy saw Jeff dressed to kill. "Where you going?" she asked out of maternal instincts.

"I don't know. Tim's driving. Maybe just hit the circuit." Jeff just wanted to get out.

The Circuit was an infamous route around the city of Williamsport touted as a pick-up destination. Even Kathy enjoyed summer nights touring the area. Girls on the take. Unfortunately, or fortunately the were no pick-ups, just fun and laughter. "Just be careful!" Kathy took a moment to pull Jeff in for a tight hug. "I love you baby."

"I love you too. Don't worry, I'll be okay. Can I borrow twenty dollars?" Jeff asked popping his bubble of selflessness.

"Honey I don't have an extra twenty. I won't get paid until tomorrow." She was short on funds herself.

"How about ten? "He wanted something.

Kathy stopped and reevaluated her cash on hand. If she gave him ten, she had $15 for gas. Payday tomorrow would be at the end of the day, and three clients to see in Sunbury. She gave in. "Okay." She pulled her wallet from her briefcase and found a ten folded in the pocket for gas money. "You make sure you're home by midnight. I don't want to worry all night. I've got to be up for work by seven. I also have talk to you before you go to bed."

"About what? Dad? "He was curious.

"No. I just have to be sure before I tell you. I gotta do some research first. I'll know by the time you get home." Kathy didn't want to tell him until her plans were definite. *Deuce had better call me tonight, or everything is off.* Kathy hated playing the waiting game.

"Whatever. I'll see you when I get back." Jeff adjusted his shirt one last time as he left to go to Tim's home, located in the Park.

"Thank you. Come again. Thanks for shopping at Mom's!" she called out as he slammed the door.

Kathy, finally alone, sat at the table and removed her shoes to rub her toes. *I don't know who came up with this shoe design, but it constrains my toes. Must have been a man.* Kathy ruminated over Deuce's not calling. Her next move took her to her bedroom where she stripped down for her needed cool shower. The day had been so hot, she dreamed of stopping at the nearest creek to dive in, clothes and all. She was extremely grateful her deodorant hadn't failed.

It was seven when she finally turned the shower on for her refreshing shower. The water was warm enough to avoid a chill, yet cool enough to off-set the heat from her body. She soaked her hair first. Leaning forward she pulled her hair up over her head and let the water run down the back of her neck. With a backward flip of the hair, she pivoted and soaked the front. The water spilled over her temples and snuck into her ears.

"Damn!" she complained as she quickly shook the water from her ears. Just then, she heard the phone ring. With a quick turn of the shower knob, Kathy grabbed her towel and raced to the phone. "Hello?"

"Well, hello to you too." The deep voice said.

Kathy's heart leapt. "Who is this?" she responded. She could never forget that voice.

"Oh, you have a lot of men calling you?" He felt a little playful.

"Deuce! Where have you been? I've been trying to get in touch with you. Didn't Betty tell you I called?" *That bitch didn't give him the message,* she thought.

"That figures. I called your boy and asked him to have you call me. I figured he wouldn't tell you. But damn, that fucking Betty never said shit. I was even down there for dinner tonight."

"I was afraid you had already gone home, forgetting me." She was relieved that her obsessive thoughts were just that.

"Are you nuts? I don't think I could ever forget you. You still thinking about you surprise?" He couldn't wait.

"You kidding me? I've gone nuts over the surprise. I hate, I'm excited, I'm confused. Where are, we going? I have to tell Jeff tonight." Kathy also needed to tell him the rules while she was gone.

"My favorite place, the mountains." Deuce pictured Kathy's excitement. *My mountain.* In his mind's eye, he saw the Dungeon.

Kathy loved to hear him talk. His deep southern dialect reminded her of her Sam Elliot. Her favorite movie starring Sam Elliot was Mask, with Cher. His deep soothing voice melted her heart. Kathy, lost in her memories, suddenly realized Deuce had stopped talking. "What?"

"…shower, then eat," was all she heard him say.

"What the hell. You watching T.V.? What are you doin'? Someone there?" Deuce stopped to think. *That damn ex better not be there again.*

"Oh, baby I got lost in your sweet voice." The light had just come on in her dark tunnel. "You said you have to get dressed before you eat. I was listening."

"Not if you were here. You know what I would eat?" Deuce didn't know it but Kathy blushed.

"Yeah, I know." She said bashfully,

"Know what?" Deuce knew Kathy was a little green and pressured her to say it.

"What you would eat?" She didn't want to play his game.

"What would I eat?" He asked smartly.

"Fuck you." She knew, but she wasn't saying it.

"That comes next." He responded cockily.

Kathy just shook her head. She had never had a conversation like that before. She began to feel dirty. "You drive me crazy."

"Not yet I'm not, but I'll do everything I can. And you'll like it." He smiled as he thought about his plan.

"Before then, where are we going? Do I need to pack a swimsuit?" Kathy pictured a resort with an indoor pool and a Jacuzzi.

"Pack it. But where we are going, you won't need it. El Natural is the best." Back woods and dilapidated roads, enables the ultimate privacy. "Do you remember that black dress you were wearing when we first met? Bring it, but don't wear it. Wear something comfortable for the drive. Something easy to slip off when we get there."

"You piss me off!" Kathy instantaneously blurted out! "I can't stop thinking about you and this damn surprise. I hate to tell you this, but," Kathy even surprised herself, "I HATE SURPRISES!"

"Whoa! I promise, no more surprises." Deuce loved her spitfire. He was amazed how his plan was taking shape. *Angie, three week and two thousand dollars; Maggie took five weeks, but only a thousand dollars and a marriage proposal. I'm glad Maggie accepted "Granny Rose's Locket" instead of an engagement ring. She was the gullible one; West Virginia's way. Kathy was the different than the last two. Rather than bleeding me for money like Angie did; Kathy exerted independence right away. Maggie needed to get out of that dusty bowl; Kathy showed no need to leave. Besides, this area is perfect. Beaver Lake takes the cake.*

If Kathy could have kicked herself at this point, she would have. "Deuce, I'm sorry, I've been obsessing. I grew to hate them; surprises that is." Kathy remembered that her first surprise led to her first divorce.

Anniversary number three. So much for three's a charm. His mistress was waiting at the restaurant to be introduced. Angelo thought we could be the threesome he wanted for his anniversary gift.

"You'll have to tell me while I'm driving. I'll pick you up around seven. You gonna be ready?" Deuce planned his last performance for his crew. Mud, which was a safety hazard, would mysteriously appear at Tibble's feet when he starts work in the morning. They called for a shower overnight, but Tibble's tarp, the one he used to cover his part of the ditch would have mysteriously disappeared. His attempts to dry the ditch would fail and Deuce would head to the boss's shack and request his layoff.

"I can't wait!" She was excited again.

"Does Jeff work tomorrow night?" Deuce hoped he wouldn't be around.

"Yep. He works all weekend, Part-timers do that." Kathy figured work would keep him busy while she was gone.

"You gonna tell him tonight that he can have the car?"

"Yep. He'll love that. Until I tell him the rules. He has a problem with authority." She'd probably piss him off again.

Deuce smiled at his success. *Right where I want her. A little wine, Granny's special recipe, and Mike's contribution, will make the ride home a breeze.* Deuce glowed with happy thoughts of his dungeon.

"Hey, I have to get dressed. You caught me in the shower. I 'm only wearing a towel." Kathy, felt a chill, and needed a reason to hang up. "I will be ready by seven, so don't be late." Kathy knew she'd be there alone after Jeff went to work, so she planned to wait out on the porch.

"I'll have my white stallion there, my lady, I'll see you then." Deuce's heart began thumping with anticipation. *In twenty-four hours, we'll be heading home. Kathy will go to sleep, and when she awakes, her surprise will be waiting. How she reacts about it, we'll have to wait and see.* Kathy had already hung up so Deuce put his phone back on the receiver and headed to the shower himself.

Chapter 18

Preparing for the Surprise

An emptiness swept over Kathy as she hung up the phone. She loved Deuce and the colloquialisms he used when he told his stories. Combined with his southern drawl, the stories he told captivated her. Living vicariously through his rendition of life kept her wanting more.

Deuce needed everything to run smooth. Friday morning, he'd have everything he owned in his car ready to go. He'd report to work as usual. Tibble would already be pissed off. He would wait around for two hours, and get his layoff then say his final good-byes to New. *There was one girl I planned to visit again. Her service was superb. New was raised redneck and would fit right in with us mountain men.*

Midnight came quickly, Deuce tipped his hat to the crowd of old-timers and climbed the steps to his room. The hall seemed darker than usual. The rain had begun, it was a cleansing rain. Granny Rose called it God's way of starting over fresh. Deuce to fell into bed, hunkered down, and gave up to the darkness.

"Slow down", Kathy yelled. "What are you trying to do, kill me?" Kathy sat beside him as they turned onto the rocky road leading home. It was a dark moonless night and when they reached his road, he began to delight in his own arrival. He closed his eyes to fantasize. Click, click, bang, and he opened his eyes. Before him was a large backhoe reaching toward him. As it did, the bucket shrunk small enough to grab his genitals. With one clank, it scooped and surrounded his balls, then grasped his penis. Fear overtook him. The backhoe stopped as Deuce searched the cab for a driver. The windshield was scratched beyond opaque. The door opened and a familiar leg with a black pump stretched down to reach the track. "Hey what the fuck are you doing?" Quickly the leg was drawn back into the cab and the door slammed shut. The engine roared to life. Deuce knew the next gear sound and knew what was coming next. Suddenly, the Lodge's fire alarm blared, pulling Deuce back to reality. Whoop, whoop, whoop! at an annoying decibel that would have awakened the dead. Deuce, still dressed, reached for his glasses, noticing sweat on his brow. "Some dream! Or, one hell of a nightmare!" He didn't move from his bed. He just waited. If no one knocked, it was a false alarm. An hour later, he was asleep.

It was only Thursday, one more day till her surprise. Upon her arrival at the office, Kathy began making plans for cold calls, premium pick-ups, and lapsed policies. It was too early for those calls, so she organized her policies, paper work and pamphlets for her next presentation.

Deuce arrived late as usual. The crew was spread out ready to descend into the pit. Welders with helpers shared their last drink of coffee in preparation for hours of welding. Deuce saw Tibble pacing near his flooded hole. He saw how anxious he was feeling by way he bitched at himself. The rain had apparently done its duty. *Granny, again you were here when I needed you.* Deuce proceeded to Tibble to see the damage he had done.

"Damn rain fucked everything up. Someone or something dragged my tarp off and it's a mess! I am so sick of this shit!" Tibble was soon to retire, but he was so greedy, he wanted to work until he dropped.

"They did warn us that black bears were in the area when we got here. How far did they drag it?" Deuce loved to watch Tibble struggle to understand what happened.

"They drug it down to the trash bin. They probably stopped there for dinner." Tibble, seeing a white helmet foreman turned and called out to him flailing his arms. He darted off to stop him to air his complaint.

Deuce got a kick out of seeing Tibble's frustration. For the thirty years, he worked on the pipeline, Tibble always found something to bitch about. Deuce was happy to oblige. Retiring ahead of him gave him the one up on him, and Deuce reveled in it. Given a chance, he would torment him relentlessly. Deuce waited patiently for his exit. A blower was placed near the pit, and the hum of air pressure became deafening. *I'm out of her!*

The work area looked abandoned, but the sound of the welders striking their arcs and melting rods to the pipe was a sound he wouldn't miss. The guys, yes, but the work, no. Deuce walked into the make-shift office. Connie, the secretary greeted him. "Connie, I got to go." He never had to say much because he personally knew The Great White Father in Tulsa. With one call to him, he had once closed a pipeline down due to safety issues.

"No problem." Connie knew and pulled the paperwork out of her desk. With a few swipes of her pen, and an official seal, Connie handed the paper to Deuce for his signature. Within minutes he was out of the parking lot heading towards Larry's Inn.

Chapter 19

Last day of Work

The couple Kathy was to present to lived eighteen miles northeast in a small town named Picture Rocks. The town was located close to Beaver Lake, and Kathy knew she had to fight her urge to go that direction. The Barton's home was on a road she could use as a short cut back to her office. She was happy to have her route back to the office planned.

Kathy, was still preparing for her presentation she heard an announcement over the intercom. *Kathy, pick- up on line one.* Since she was the only Kathy there, she automatically picked up the phone. "American General. This is Kathy how may I help you?"

"Kathy, this is Gene Barton. We have an appointment scheduled with you today at three."

"Yes Mr. Burton, is there something I can help you with?" She hoped it wouldn't be a difficult request.

"My wife was called in to work today and she wants me to reschedule our meeting until Monday. Would that be a problem?"

"No Mr. Barton, not at all. That happens to nurses all the time. Would you like to set a time?"

"Let's keep it at three. Will that work for you?" Mr. Barton asked.

"By looking at my schedule; I can pencil you in easily." Kathy made sure she stifled her disappointment. After he hung up, Kathy realized the day was already a bust. This was the only chance to sell a new policy, receive a commission, and get referrals. But since no one knew, she decided to take the afternoon off to find a sundress for the trip. Kathy continued the morning searching for lapsed policies to arrange meetings for the following week.

Lunch time, appeared quickly. For lunch, Kathy decided a trip to the Mall would kill two birds with one stone. A sundress for the trip she would get at Sears, and her meal today would be a simple burger from McDonalds. Afterwards, she would spend the day at home getting ready. Before she left, she grabbed her check. This paycheck included commissions from the week before. *She would have enough to give Jeff money for the weekend too.* Kathy knew Jeff would need extra for incidentals and food. Everything could be taken care of at the Lycoming Mall.

The heat from the August day was oppressive. *Grandma would say It's close.* The humidity was suffocating and there was no wind moving. Kathy bumped her air-conditioning up to the max as soon as she entered her home. Even though it had been running all day, the trailer she lived in felt like an oven set on low. With bags in hand, Kathy went directly to her room to pack for her trip.

Kathy chose a zebra printed suitcase for the trip. She chose the clothing she wanted to take and laid it out on the bed. The first row, tops, then pants. Beside those items, she placed her underclothes, swimming suit and personal items like perfumes, facial cream, and soap. She wanted to be prepared for anything.

Jeff working a double shift, so she would leave the car keys and extra money at a prearranged spot. Jeff knew she would be leaving money, but would be shocked at the one-hundred-dollar bill. *Spend it wisely baby,* she thought as she laid it and the keys on top of the refrigerator.

Kathy decided to get showered and dressed for her trip. The sundress was a cotton pull-over, with soft multi-colored flowers, predominately rose in color. Her most daring buy was the pair of white thong underwear. This was something she had never worn. She felt a sting in the crack of her ass. It would take time to get used that discomfort. *I don't know how young girls can stand wearing these underpants!* she thought readjusting them. *I hope Deuce appreciates the effort.*

Chapter 20

Tying Loose Ends

Larry's Inn was crowded with breakfast and brunch patrons. New saw Deuce immediately and sat him at a table close to the bar. "What? Coffee and Jack now? Or, do you want to wait for your food?" New was prompt.

"Coffee and jack now, then get me the big breakfast. Thanks." Deuce glanced around the room. Everyone loved this Inn. New provided excellent service and excellent food. This was the only place he found on the road that he hated to leave.

New arrived quickly with his coffee then disappeared into the kitchen with his order. The hot, toxic liquid, was meant to be sipped, so he left to cool while he smoked his cigarette. Quietly he pondered. *I wish we could leave earlier.* He pictured the dungeon and Kathy waiting there for him. *Dressed in a flowing white gown, she would always be eager for my return. Kathy will love being with me. If she lasts, she will see OUR land, the caves, and the bunker. I know she'll LOVE it!* Deuce surprised himself. He knew it was possible, but those feelings had been squashed. *That's nuts! Granny would smack me upside the head if she heard that. Per Granny Rose, I needed to be on guard around women. Money hungry controllers. If she were here, I wonder what she'd find wrong with Kathy.* Granny's influence over Deuce was apparent. Granny raised him after his mom and dad were killed. *Me and my brothers hunted and fished daily to put food on the table. Four crazy boys for one women to raise. Rules were number one, especially after Grandpa was killed. Her word was law. Buster took care of that. Granny's use of Buster prosecuted violators.*

"Where are you?" New asked as she set his food down in front of him. "You leaving today? I heard they are laying-off." New hated to see him leave. She had grown to love this Southern Gentleman. She loved his dialect paired with his respect. Never once had he over-stepped.

"Yep, one of them. Going to be headin' home." Deuce knew he had to wish her good-bye, but the words didn't reach him. Instead, Deuce gave her a tip to say it for him. Beaver Lake brought him luck; good people and that special one he would be taking home with him.

"Since this is you last breakfast here, we want you to enjoy it on the house." New nearly teared up as she finished placing his food down.

"No need of that. It's good. Better than I've found." Deuce hated taking anything from anybody.

"No choice. Just eat it. How is the coffee? Need another?" New became flustered and left to help other tables.

"No…" Deuce watched as New made herself busy. *Boy she's upset.* Deuce gladly ate the large breakfast. Eggs. Sausage, bacon, hash browns, and pancakes spread over two plates, this was one of his favorites. He quickly gulped the coffee down in one shot, then started on the eggs and bacon. The rest slid down just as easy, as the Jack lubricated his palate. Upon finishing, Deuce looked to find New. As he looked around the room, he noticed travel mugs adorned with the Beaver Lake logo. "*I need them,*" he thought. "NEW!" he called when he saw her emerge from the kitchen. "I'm ready." New knew his code, then he added, "Grab me two of those Beaver Lake cups."

New heard and responded immediately, grabbing two mugs as she passed by. "You want another coffee?" New wanted him to stay longer.

"Can't. Gotta long drive ahead of me, so I gotta pass. I'm gonna stop at Wally World and get some munchies then haul ass. It's nearly an eight-hour drive!" Deuce knew he wasn't stopping there, instead he knew of a store where he could buy the wine for the trip. Armed with the Mugs, Deuce's plan was nearly complete.

Chapter 21

Ready for the Surprise

Kathy was waiting on the couch watching CMTV. Country music calmed her and excited her depending on the song. The time was near, and she had already brought her packed suitcase from her room. Five more minutes and she would station herself on the front porch. Butterflies inhabited her stomach. The steel nerves of a teenager, were exactly what she felt. Never had she felt this ominous feeling. Was it fear or excitement? Either way she trusted Deuce with her heart.

The time had come. She stood and readjusted her dress. Grabbing her suitcase, she walked out on the porch, pulling the door shut behind her. Bea was watered and fed before she left, and the door was locked. She was ready to go. The day was still warm and the sun still bright. Not noticing, Kathy wondered if Deuce's car had air-conditioning. The trip without it would be torture.

Deuce pulled into Kathy's drive just minutes later. Unbuckling his seat belt, he opened his door and stepped out. "The Stallion has arrived!" he announced. "Ready to go to the moon and back?" Deuce bowed as a Southern Gentleman.

"Can you grab my bag for me?" Kathy was impressed, but didn't want to show it.

Deuce complied and grabbed her bag from her and tossed it in the back seat. In a gentlemanly fashion, Deuce proceeded ahead of Kathy and opened the passenger door. Before she had a chance to crawl in, he grabbed her and planted a soft kiss on her mouth. Kathy responded in turn. No words were exchanged as Kathy slid in, Deuce closed the door, and proceeded to mount his white stallion and begin the trip towards his mountain.

Chapter 22

Meanwhile Back at the Farm

It had been nearly three years since Margret's body was found. It had been difficult to discover her identity. A woman from Texas found in this part of Clay County was still a classified as Jane Doe. Rusty had ruminated over it since. Choosing to clear his mind, Rusty decided to ride Jasmine along the paths of the hillside. Jasmine had been retired from police work shortly after Margret was found. Today, she enjoyed the leisurely life of grazing in her pasture and riding through the woods of Clay and Kanawha Counties. Rusty loved that part of his life; the other was challenging.

Rusty remained on the Clay County Police force despite Jasmine's retirement. He missed the walking and climbing he and Jasmine did. Pool-hounds frequented the local bars, but Rusty found a local Mom and Pop Casino/Bar to be his favorite. Everyone knew him and his reputation. He felt accepted and loved by all the regulars.

Rusty selected the path where he had found Margret's locket years ago. He had chosen this path for every ride ever since. Margret's mystery had become a big part of his heart way more than any other police case. Somewhere deep down, he blamed himself for her death. Riding the trail kept her murder in his thoughts. *She was a beauty. Whoever did that to her will pay. I don't know who or where, but it will come to fruition.* Rusty believed in Karma. Many times, perps were caught due to their own Karma. Perps ran from justice and often landed behind bars due to minor infractions. Many called that karma.

The sun was peeking through the trees, casting beams of light across the forest floor. Just ahead was the field Rusty loved, and where he allowed Jasmine to run at her own pace. Following his usual routine, he packed Jasmine an apple, him a sandwich, and bottle of water. Rusty held the reins tighter when Jasmine increased her pace to a trot as she approached the field. Allowing her to set her own pace, Rusty not only held the reins light enough to allow her to run, but also to keep himself steady. Jasmine started her gallop, as she crossed the open field.

While Jasmine galloped through the field, as usual, a feral dog appeared, barking wildly. At first it was a protective bark, but Rusty pulled out a treat, it became more of an excited bark. Rusty would always have raw meat for him, worried he would starve. He called him Dog. Otis responded to Rusty as another master, and Jasmine allowed him to familiarize himself with her. Friends? No, just two animals respecting their master. Rusty understood that and never failed to reward his servants.

Jasmine slowed and her perspiration began to show. Otis, who instinctively followed, slowed alongside of the running duo. Anticipating his reward, Otis made sure they wouldn't get away. Rusty noticed him only minutes after the run began, and saw he had lost weight. Pulling back gently on Jasmine's reins, Rusty asked her to stop. Otis slowed, but began to excitedly run in circles and bark.

Rusty, dismounted Jasmine and pulled the bag of food from his saddle bag. "Dog, here!" he called. Pulling the leftover meat from the bag, Otis was there instantly. "Here, you need this." Rusty tossed the meat towards him, which barely hit the ground before it was consumed. A bottle of water was the next to be offered. Rusty used the plastic bag that held the meat, to hold the water for Otis. Otis drew near and lapped up the water quickly. Rusty turned to Jasmine and offered her an apple, as Otis finished his water.

Otis finished his water, wagging his tail in gratification. As he approached Rusty, hoping for more, his ears perked to a barely audible scream. Rusty also heard the same noise, and instinctively knew it was nothing natural to the area. He stopped and waited for further sounds. Nothing followed, but Rusty couldn't let it go. Otis was apparently the same, and took off running down the hill towards a tree line. Rusty stood to watch as he disappeared. *Should I follow?* He considered. *This is that old man's land. Maybe he's home, finally.* Rusty had tried numerous time to catch him home between jobs, He knew he was a pipeliner and was never without a job for very long. He knew if he wanted to talk to him, he would have to visit him quickly.

Rusty considered going home to get his Police I.D., but decided to ride down as a neighbor. wanting permission to ride his land. He knew he had been trespassing when he brought Jasmine to run in his field, but he had never been able to connect with him. Even after the locket was found at the entrance of the trail on his land, every attempt to speak with him failed. *Here's my chance. I need to go. I'll go around and come up the drive. That way I can stop him before he leaves.* With that, Rusty climbed back onto Jasmine's saddle and tipped the reins left to ask Jasmine to go down the hill. Hesitantly, Jasmine began a slow canter into unfamiliar ground. As Rusty rode, he began to create his introduction.

Chapter 23

Unaware

Deuce arrived back to the trailer as the sun began to sink over the mountain's horizon. The valleys experienced shorter days of direct sunlight because of the different mountain heights. Coming up the mountain through the valley, the road snaked by streams which were created by springs flowing through the limestone. It was all beautiful during the sunshine of the day, but the sun set by the time he was three quarters of the way home. He had gotten all the groceries he needed in town, but since he was a well know figure in the town, he would often stop to converse which made his absence longer. As he approached the gate to his compound, his mind turned to Kathy. *She should still be out. But, after the food is put away, I think it's time for her surprise.*

Deuce suddenly realized that Otis hadn't met him at the gate, especially since he had always brought a treat home with him. Otis' favorite treat was a bone-in fatty beef roast and he usually obliged him.

Deuce finished putting away his groceries and went to an old braided circular rug in the living room. He pulled it away to reveal a trap door with an inverted handle. He lifted the door sending a puff of dust throughout the room. Kathy began to come alive realizing she was unable to move. A loud scream pierced the air as she saw Deuce descend the ladder from the trap door.

"Deuce! What's going on? Get me out of this. I'm stuck." Kathy's heart was racing. Still suffering some effects from the wine, she told herself, *Oh God, I will never drink again. Please help me get out of here.*

Her attention turned to Deuce, who nonchalantly began to remove his pants. Already erect, Kathy knew he was responsible for everything. "What the fuck are you doing? Why?"

Deuce, without responding, turned to a wall holding a plethora of whips and sex toys. He grabbed a whip made of a thin leather braid. This was a Pig Whip, specially designed to keep a pig in line. This was hanging among the Dungeon Medieval whips, Western Bull Whips, and Bikers' Get Back whips. Deuce always used the pig whip first. He thought this whip was more frightening. He also grabbed a ball gag before turning back to Kathy.

"Now you know, this is what I like. I'm sorry I had to do it this way, but I know it's the only true way to reveal it. You would have never even looked at me twice knowing this. So, trust me, I won't hurt you. I love you and don't ever want to lose you." He approached Kathy who laid quietly in fearful shock. "Relax, you'll love this'" Deuce the proceeded to lay the items he acquired on the floor beside him then grabbed the swing and pulled Kathy close enough that he could insert himself into his reward.

Kathy winced not from pain, but disgust. To avoid the reality of the situation, Kathy mentally removed herself. *God, I haven't talked to you since Sunday school. Please forgive me. Keep my family safe. I'm so sorry for the end of my marriage. I should have done more. Keep Jeff safe and protect him in my absence. Please don't let him hate me for leaving him. And if you can, and it's your will, help me get out of here!*

As the smothering summer heat began to filter into the dungeon, Deuce's sweat gathered. Kathy laid quietly as he continued reaping his reward. He used her dress as a sweat mop. Kathy didn't notice. She was imagining that she was soaking up the sun on a beach in Wildwood. She learned this method from a Sociology course in college. She never thought she would ever use it. Yes, she felt what was happening, but chose to go back to the only beach she had ever visited. The sun was warm and the ocean water cool. Oh, she wanted to go back again!

At the rear door, Otis scratched to get in. Deuce was just ready to explode so he ignored his call. Swinging Kathy quicker, his climax shivered down his legs. Grabbing on to the swings straps, he held himself steady as the quivering stopped. "Baby, you're the best!" He mostly meant, *At least you didn't fight me on this.* He then used a towel on a bench in the center of the room and put his pants back on. "The next time I'll give you the pleasure. It wasn't that bad, was it?"

Kathy didn't answer, still laying on a beach in Wildwood. She feared returning to reality. Going back would lead to the grief of losing a fantasy. *I wish the ocean would sweep me away.*

Deuce decided to let Otis into the dungeon; "You stay here. I'm gonna get you some beef."

Walking up to Kathy, he stopped to readjust her dress. Putting his hand on her leg, he said, "I'll be right back. I'm gonna get Otis the meat bought him. I also got us dinner; pizza. I gotta warm it up in the microwave; then I'll bring it down. We gotta talk. I'll get you off the swing too," without a whisper from Kathy at the beach, he turned to climb the ladder.

Otis heard it first and they both froze. Quickly turning towards Kathy, Deuce grabbed the ball-gag and forced Kathy off her beach. His quickness and accuracy showed experience as he stuffed the gag in her mouth. Kathy's eyes widened out of fright!

"Shhh!" Deuce commanded, as he heard a knock on the door. Otis was barking. Deuce straightened his pants and climbed the ladder, closing the trap door, and covering it again with the rug.

"On my way!" he called.

Chapter 24

The End was Near

Rusty heard the call from a male voice inside and knew it had to be the owner of the white Cavalier parked at the side of the trailer. He hoped he hadn't interrupted him in the bathroom. He knew that was never good. Coming up the drive through the opened gate assured him he was home.

The door opened with a tight squeak, as if it hadn't been opened too often. A man with graying auburn hair and mustache opened the door with a delightful smile. "What can I do for ya?" he asked.

Rusty instinctively smiled back and reached his hand to introduce himself. "I'm Rusty Jackson and I live in Beaumont, just a few properties from your property line. As you can see, I own that Appaloosa. Her name is Jasmine. I've been hoping to catch you home for years. I know you are a man who works all over the country laying pipe, but I've never had a chance to catch you home."

Deuce heard what he was saying but was eager for him to leave. "So, what can I help you with?"

"Well sir, for the past three years I have occasionally ridden Jasmine up a trail on your land leading to that beautiful open field. I want to apologize for trespassing and want to ask formal permission. I did no damage, and never rode on the land when it was soft from rain."

"Well, I see no reason you shouldn't be allowed. Someone needs to enjoy it. And your right I am traveling the country working." Deuce never knew anyone was using that field. It wasn't like he did, so he had no qualms about it.

A high-pitched moan came from within. Rusty heard it, there was no denying it. "My dog Otis. I always bring him a special treat when I get home. He's just one weird dog. He moans out of satisfaction." Deuce walked out the door closing it behind him. "Let's look at Jasmine," he said as he walked past Rusty toward Jasmine. He wanted to redirect his attention after the noise.

Rusty showed no sign of concern after he heard the moan. He did however know Otis didn't make that noise. With all his police training and experience, he knew how to show no concern. But, deep down, he knew. After that brief scream, and his knowledge of Dog, there was something going on he was hiding.

Deuce walked around Jasmine as if he knew horses. He stroked her neck, patted her rump, and stood examining her from nose to tail. Rusty said nothing waiting for his evaluation. "Beautiful. She is beautiful. It looks like you keep her in great condition. Have you had her since she was a foal?"

"No, just for the past fifteen years. She's 18 now." Rusty loved that horse.

"I'll be doggone. She's a beauty! Yes, you can ride my land. Someone's gotta use it." Deuce felt no concerns. *"Here's a nice boy asking permission. That's rare now-a-days."*

Rusty shook Deuce's hand one final time and mounted Jasmine to ride home. Deuce stood to watch him leave. With a wave good-bye, Rusty nudged Jasmine to pick up her speed to leave. Rusty had a lot of thinking to do, and needed to go back to his office to review his notes. *There's something fishy about this man. I know he lied to me, and now I'm worried about that scream. I have to check this out.*

It took an hour to get to his office in Clay. The office was empty, but always open for police work. The first place Rusty turned was the cold case files. Margret was Rusty's first stop. He reviewed where and how she was found. The distance from Deuce's land was significant. The next part was to look for associations to pipelines being laid in Texas near her home. This took some time. At that time, there were numerous pipelines laid to accommodate the numerous Oil and Gas Companies. At final count, there were three. Now he looked at the names of each company involved in laying pipe. Companies came out of Oklahoma, Washington, and Georgia. He started to look up main office numbers for each, to make inquiries as to whether Deuce had worked for them at that time.

Since it was Saturday, Rusty knew he had to wait until Monday morning. *I hope there are no other victims. I just can't get that scream out of my head. I just need a reason to go back.* Rusty hated to give up so soon, but closing time came and went. He packed all the important items needed for his investigation into his briefcase and Rusty secured his notes for Monday. Before then, he made a mental note to visit Deuce's land on Jasmine in the morning. If there is another scream, there will be a Welfare Check. This allows police to avoid the 4th Amendment Right and enter a home on probable cause. Rusty knew this, as he had done Welfare Checks for children at risk.

Deuce went back down to the dungeon to take care of Kathy. She laid quietly, without movement and eyes closed. Tears flowed effortlessly from the sides of her eyes. Deuce approached her, noticing her tears. Quickly he began to remove the Ball Gag. "Promise not to scream? I'm not going to hurt you; I promise. I really do think you were meant for me. I never felt this way before. I think you are the one Granny Rose hoped I'd find."

Kathy took no solace in his words or touch. During his absence, her mind raced. *Why didn't I see this? What's wrong with me. Am I that desperate? My son was right; I am a whore. Or is he just a predator? I wonder how many others he did this to. God, I pray for your forgiveness. I know I haven't talked with you in a long time, but I pray you will help me, if it is your will. Please watch over my son. I don't know what he will do without me.* Tears flowed waiting on a wail of pain. Kathy held it in as the Ball Gag came out of her mouth.

Deuce pulled Kathy's dress up, exposing her to him again. "I'll make you feel better," he said as he knelt to orally stimulate her. He had used this method in the past, so he knew she had no choice except to have an orgasm. He uses the guilt of having an orgasm to manipulate them into cooperating. *They never realized it was out of their control, and only a biological function of the body, aiding in fertilization.* With tears flowing, Kathy needed to blow her nose, but no way to do it. The stimulation began, so she turned her head and tried to blow her nose on to her bare arm. The warm snot was more then she thought and ran down beneath her arm pit. "Please help me. I had to blow my nose, and made a mess."

Deuce heard her and stopped what he had started. He stood to look. "Damn!" was all he said as he turned to grab the towel he used earlier. Being sure to use the clean end, he wiped Kathy's arm off the placed it over her nose. "Blow." As Kathy cleared her nose, "You know, it'll be okay. Just quit fighting it. I told you; I won't hurt you. In fact, I want to pleasure you. Just give me a chance."

"Deuce, why did you do this? I trusted you. I would have never thought you would do this."

"Kathy, I found you and never want to lose you. I was serious when I told you I had never found anyone like you in all my travels. But, I knew you'd run if you found out about my sexual oddities. I guess it's called sexual sadism. I hate that term, but it's just the way I am. I haven't hurt you much, have I?"

Kathy couldn't believe what he said. "Hurt me? What the fuck are talking about? It hurt just waking up in this position. Physically and mentally. I can't believe you kidnapped me."

"Kidnap? No, we went for a romantic weekend to the mountains. This is my mountain."

"Why wouldn't you tell me we were coming here?" She was confused.

"I didn't want any interruptions. Besides, I knew you'd never come if you had known why."

He was right; Kathy would have ended their relationship if she had known. In her opinion, he had never shown any mental illness. But it was too late. Now she needed to rely on her education, and experience working in a State Psychiatric Hospital to save her own life. She started to evaluate her situation and form a plan for escape.

"Deuce, I'm hungry. I need a drink too. Can you get me out of this and get me something? I'd really appreciate it."

"Pizza should be ready soon. I put it in the microwave. I picked some up while I was out. You want a beer with It?"

"Sure. But, can you get me out of this? My shoulders hurt. Please?"

Deuce responded quickly to her request. He truly didn't want to hurt her, but his proclivity to his desires controlled him. Releasing her wrists first, "Don't try getting up until I release your ankles and help you up." With that statement, he released her completely and lifted her from the swing. Placing her in a standing position, he held her steady as she regained he balance. "Sit over here on the bench; I'll go get the food."

After Kathy made it to the bench, Deuce climbed the ladder to the kitchen. Kathy glanced around the dungeon and saw whips and sex toys hanging on the wall. She shook her head and placed her hand on her forehead, placing he elbow on her leg, looking down toward the floor. *My god, what did I get myself into?*

It was nine o'clock when Rusty got home. He ruminated over his need to figure a way to get back to Deuce's home and check on that scream he had lied about. *God, please let it be nothing. If you want me in there, help me find a way. Don't let another woman be hurt.*

Night spread over the trailer quickly as they finished their pizza and beer. The dungeon was built with cinder blocks. It was cold and there was no sleeping area, so Deuce asked, "I have a bed upstairs; do you think you can climb the ladder? Or do you want to walk around to the front door?"

She thought fresh air would help so she responded quickly. "I'm cold. Can we go outside. Maybe we can grab my suitcase so I can change.

"We gotta pass the car anyways. I'll grab it on the way." Deuce put out his hand out to help her up, then continued to hold her arm as he led her out the door.

Kathy felt the warmth of the August night as she stepped through the door. The darkness obscured her view. She did, however, see the trailer she had been under. Nearby was an old building she assumed was once a Hen House. Four limestone columns were set up as legs to the house, and showed its age. The trailer itself looked to be old as well. *So much for his lie of having a beautiful home. Money doesn't mean shit if you have to live like this!*

Deuce led her to the car where he pulled her suitcase out of the backseat, He held her hand firmly as he walked her to the front door. He opened it and continued to lead her to the back bedroom. There, he finally released her hand, dropped the suitcase and said, "I'll let you change. I'll be out getting another beer. You want one?"

"Sure. Got any more pot?" Kathy was hoping it would help her escape mentally. The inside of the trailer was as bad as the outside. The only difference was she was warmer. She saw the bed was sagging in the center, showing its age.

"That's my girl! Yep, I'll roll us a joint while I'm gone. I'll be right back." Deuce pulled the door closed as he left.

Kathy noticed the trailer was much warmer than the block room she had been kept in. Out of sheer mental exhaustion, Kathy collapsed on the bed. It was soft. She looked at the ceiling, which was covered in spider webs. Her mind went home, hoping Jeff was safe and in bed. *I wish things could have been different. Jeff deserves better than this.*

Deuce returned to find Kathy laying on the bed without changing. "You decide not to change?" he asked as he placed the beers on a side table. With a flick of his Bic, he lit the joint. "This is really good quality pot that I had in my freezer. You're gonna like it." He took a long drag. Coughing, he handed it to her.

Kathy happily took it and drew a hard toke, coughing as Deuce did. She felt it immediately. Wanting more, she toked again after her coughing subsided. The next draw was slower, but she coughed again.

"Whoa! you all right?" Deuce took the joint from her as she looked at him with glassy eyes.

"Much better." Kathy squeezed out a smile. It felt better, but reality hovered over her. *Maybe another beer would help.* She hated beer, but the alcoholic buzz was what she wanted. "Deuce, can I have another beer?"

"Well sure!" he said, liking the sounds of that. "On its way baby."

After Deuce left the room, Kathy looked around for a telephone. Sadly, the was none. Deuce had left the joint in an ashtray near the door, so Kathy decided, *one more hit can't hurt!* So, pulling herself up, she got the snubbed out joint. One problem, no lighter. She walked to the side table and not seeing a lighter, she opened the table drawers. There on top of papers, laid an S&M Magazine. She placed her hand under all the papers and felt around. Suddenly, she felt a gun. Scared, she pulled her hand out and slammed the drawer closed. *I think I'll wait!* she thought as she hopped back on the bed.

Deuce returned, carrying two beers. "I see you got the joint. Let me light that for you." Deuce pulled out his Bic and flicked it for her. "Kinda' nice being able to smoke at will, isn't it?"

After drinking the beers and finishing the joint, the two laid down on the bed. Kathy expected another round of lurid advances, but Deuce only talked of his farm, his Granny Rose, and how happy he was to find Kathy. With no response from Kathy, Deuce saw she was asleep. *Thank you, Granny. You knew what I needed.* In minutes, he also succumbed to sleep.

Rusty tossed and turned all night. His mind raced as he thought about his trip back to Deuce's land. *I have to come up with a feasible plan. I gotta call Doc, Cummings, and Taylor. I'll call the office at eight. I'll grab my SAT Phone.*

Rusty arose around seven a.m. and after a donut and a cup of coffee, gathered everything he needed for the trip to Deuce's field. After calling the office, Rusty knew his comrades would jump into action. Brinkman from Clendenin would also be involved, since Deuce's address was Clendenin, Clay County, West Virginia, it was mandatory to bring him into the investigation. Doc would be the one calling him.

After mounting Jasmine, Rusty allowed her to decide when she was ready. This time she sensed it was time to work, and she began to trot towards their destination. Instincts and training made her invaluable. They reached the field in no time, then Jasmine stopped for a break. Jasmine glistening with sweat, needed to be watered before calling the Office.

Pulling the SAT phone from his saddle bag, Rusty dialed the office number, not knowing who would answer. He hoped it was Taylor; Cummings panicked too quickly.

"Clay County Police Department, how can I help you?" Officer Cummings answered, sounding official.

"Cummings this is Jackson, do you know where Taylor is?" Rusty hoped.

"Taylor!" he called. "Jackson wants you."

A minute passed. "Yeah?" he said. Taylor finally responded.

"I got something to tell you. You sitting down?" Rusty wanted to prepare Taylor for his suspicions.

"Hey, if you're pregnant, I want a blood test." Between them all, Taylor was the wittiest.

"I have to tell you. Yesterday I went riding up to Deuce's field like always. His dog came up as usual, and I fed him again. I heard a scream coming from the direction of his home, so I went down. He was home, so I asked permission to ride his land. When we were standing at his door, I heard a muffled strange noise."

"So?" Taylor was getting annoyed.

"So, he lied to me about the muffled noise. You know, I know his dog. I feed him all the time. Deuce said it was the dog eating. There is no way he makes that noise. Someone made that noise, and screamed. I'm here on his land, field now. I think we need to do a Welfare Check. There's more, but I think it's best not to wait. What do you think?"

Sheriff Taylor froze in thought. *Who do I call?* Sheriff Taylor knew Deuce. He had served in Vietnam at the same time. And in the 70's everyone had their limits tested. Deuce was hardcore. As a sniper in the Army, Taylor knew Deuce was well armed and a crack shot. He needed an equal, even if it took 10 men. But to take him one on one on his turf, would take help. *Brinkman!* Clendenin's new chief is a Vet. He served in the army as well.

"What do you think? There's more, but I must wait until Monday to verify it. I think there is someone there. Can we use the Welfare check?" Rusty stood in the field beside Jasmine. She waited patiently as he talked.

The Broken Roads End

"Let me call Brinkman. He'll be more than willing to help." Taylor hung up without saying goodbye, and immediately dialed the number for the Clendenin Police department.

The phone rang at the desk of Dale Brinkman, Chief of police, at the Clendenin Town Hall. Brinkman immediately picked up. "Clendenin Police," was all he said.

"Dale, Sheriff Taylor from Clay. I need your help." Sheriff Taylor filled Brinkman in on the situation and probability.

"Deuce? You serious? You know how well he is loved around here. Are you sure?"

"One hundred percent" Taylor responded.

"How soon you want me there? Brinkman was ready to roll.

"Jackson is on his land now. We can meet on the road right before his drive. We will be Rusty's backup." Replied Taylor.

"It'll take me 15 minutes to get there. You ready now?"

"I gotta call Doc, but Cummings and I are ready."

"Let's roll." Brinkman stood, grabbed his gun, checked to make sure it was loaded, and holstered up. In less than a minute he was in his cruiser and heading to the rendezvous.

The forces were all called and responding. Rusty knew he could count on them, especially in this situation. He continued talking with Taylor after he was informed that the force was on their way. The plan was to make it a friendly visit, ask some questions, and attempt to be invited into his home for a beer. It was still early in the day, but from what he had discovered, Deuce was an alcoholic, and his drink of choice, beer. Rusty was to meet Taylor at the entrance to his drive, where he would have a twelve pack of Bud Light to use as a ploy. A Thank you for allowing him and Jasmine to use the land, and a way into his good graces.

The forces met at the entrance to his driveway. Luckily, the drive was hidden from his trailer. Otis, however was there to meet the group. Rusty automatically pulled out a treat for Otis and offered it to him. As Rusty remounted Jasmine, he placed the plastic bag around the saddle's horn. With a whistle to Otis, Rusty began his ride towards Deuce's home.

The plan for the group was to await the signal, then walk up the drive, and remain out of sight. As per Rusty's description of Deuce's land, an old barn would be the point of attack.

When rusty reached the front of Deuce's home, he called out, "Deuce!" he waited. "Deuce, I brought you a thank you gift!"

Deuce and Kathy, still in the bed, were alerted by the first call. "Shhh." Using his hand, he covered her mouth firmly. He whispered, "Stay here and be quiet." Reaching into the drawer of the side table, Deuce pulled out his revolver, checked it, and tucked it in the back of his pants. "You best watch yourself." The glare in his eyes alarmed Kathy.

It only took half a New York minute to open the door with his infamous grin. "Back again. You do love the land."

"Yes, sir I do. Jasmine too! I do bribe her with apples, but it sure helps keep her healthy! I wanted to thank you for your kindness and offer you this twelve pack of Bud Light."

"You hadn't oughta. I'm just glad someone can enjoy the land. I'm hardly ever home. I work all over, so I'm gone mostly" Deuce appreciated his offer. *You don't hear much of people bringing beer. They want to come drink, but usually to drink my beer.*

"Well, I never. You know, there aren't many like you anymore. Thanks." Deuce happily walked toward Rusty to retrieve the beer.

As Deuce walk toward Rusty and Jasmine, Rusty motioned Jasmine to turn her back to Deuce. "Man, she's skittish today." Rusty explained.

"I heard that. My Grandpa raised horses back in the day." Deuce reached up and patted Jasmine's rump.

Rusty motioned Jasmine to buck then subdue. This was a special trick he used when she was still on the force.

In one swift movement, Jasmine bucked Deuce hard enough to drop him on his back. Tuning 180 degrees, Jasmine placed her right front hoof over his genitals. She applied her weight just until he started to verbally acknowledge the pressure, then held it there despite his scream of pain.

Rusty pulled his badge out of his breast pocket, showed a warrant and said, Anthony Paul Rose, A.K.A Deuce, this is a warrant to search your property, for the welfare of all." Rusty then whistled loudly and from around the backside of the barn came, Clay County's Sheriff Taylor, Police Officer Cumming, Chief Brinkman of Clendenin, and Doctor Holmes, the Clay County Coroner, all with guns drawn.

Kathy, peering out through the window, and aware of the situation, flew to the front door, with her hands in the air and exclaimed, "Thank God you're here. This son-of-a-bitch kidnapped me and raped me! Thank God, Thank God!" Her tears turned to tears of joy.

"You the one I heard scream yesterday?" Rusty left Jasmine and ran to Kathy's side as she collapsed into a pile. Rusty stooped to pick her up into his arms. "You're okay now." Rusty motioned to Doc to come check on Kathy. Deuce was still left moaning in agony, as Jasmine held her position

Doc immediately took his stethoscope out and asked, "Are you hurt? Bleeding anywhere?" and placed the stethoscope to her chest.

Brinkman, Taylor, and Cummings surrounded Deuce and grasped his arms as Jasmine released him.

"He's got a gun!" Kathy called out.

Brinkman flipped Deuce over onto his stomach firmly and snatched the revolver from the back of his pants. "Anthony Paul Rose, A.K.A. Deuce, you are under arrest for, kidnap, rape, resisting arrest, attempted murder, and whatever else we can throw against you, and stick." Deuce was cuffed and sat-up to wait for Cummings to return with the Police car. "You know deuce, I would never had believed this, but here it is. You have the right to remain silent…" His rights were read to him, he said he understood, as Cumming arrived to place him in the car.

Kathy wept. Her nightmare was ending. She thought he was everything she ever wanted; The Southern Gentleman whose dialect enchanted her. She never knew there were men like Deuce, who for psychological messed up reasons, could do something so heinous. Kathy realized her vulnerability came from remaining in the loveless marriage for so long, her judgment was warped. She knew she couldn't share this with Jeff, but she hated lying to him. Her story would be: Deuce went home to West Virginia, and no, there were no plans to see him again. Then Kathy would then change the subject to Bea and her homecoming.

Chapter 25

Epilogue

Deuce was transferred to County Lock-up. Monday, Rusty checked with the companies around the area of Margret's home in Texas, and found the connection. He then checked the National Missing Persons data base, compared it to Deuce's where he had worked, and found a missing woman named Angela A. Wilson. She disappeared from the Anchorage Alaska area. Rusty knew it was over, but decided to compare other missing persons in the area to Deuce's M.O. for possible connections. Rusty planned to send Kathy home on a plane, the arranging a car to take her home. A rape kit was performed and pictures taken. The entire farm was searched and more evidence was obtained.

"Tomorrow we'll take the cadaver dog up to the property to search for Angela. I'm just glad he will never be able to kill and rape again."

Acknowledgments

I would like to thank Larry Dale Taylor for his love, patience, and inspiration. For a year, he put up with my working on this book. I want to dedicate this book to him. He was and always will be the love of my life, and I hope all who read this know the love he had for everyone. He was my pipeliner.

Dona Leah Strayer-Cillo, my sister, Ghost Writer, and final editor, I want to thank you for your dedication. Your skills polished my writing and gave me a better understanding of the job you undertook. I love you forever.

Thanks to Sherry Jane Sharpnack-Eaton, my cousin and life-long friend. Your spirit inspired your character in this book. I will always remember our personal adventures at Beaver Lake. I am glad your family has maintained our Grandparents' home and maintained our family's presence on the Lake which was once owned by our Great-Great Grandfather Augustus Sones. The Lodge continues to flourish and dinners there together will create precious memories.

Many thanks to Toni Eck, Barbours, PA, photographer, for her photo used on the book's cover. She has been a friend since Creative Writing class.

Clendenin, West Virginia still holds a place in my heart. The people there are friends for life, and are always welcome me despite years of separation. I love you all.

Mostly, I give praise and thanks to God for the power to know the story presented in the book. Without his guidance, I would have never had finished it. Thank you Lord for your patience.

About the Author

From a small town in Pennsylvania, Montoursville, which became famous due to Flight 800 IN 1986, I spent most summers challenging myself to read as many books as possible as I laid in the sun as a teenager. The love for reading came from my mother. When I reached college age, I began in Photo-Journalism, becoming the Photo Editor in my first year. I continued learning, and now have a B.A. in Psychology and Elementary Education. I grew up at Beaver Lake, Muncy Valley, PA in the 1970's since my Great Grandparents had once owned it and lived at the Lodge.

Made in the USA
Monee, IL
21 September 2022

14174724R00094